Thomas Middleton's Women Beware Women: A Retelling

David Bruce

Published by David Bruce, 2023.

This is a work of fiction. Similarities to real people, places, or events are entirely coincidental.

THOMAS MIDDLETON'S WOMEN BEWARE WOMEN: A RETELLING

First edition. April 28, 2023.

Copyright © 2023 David Bruce.

ISBN: 979-8223614722

Written by David Bruce.

Table of Contents

Dedication

The Doing of Good Deeds is Important

As a free person, you can choose to live your life as a good person or as a bad person. To be a good person, do good deeds. To be a bad person, do bad deeds. If you do good deeds, you will become good. If you do bad deeds, you will become bad. To become the person you want to be, act as if you already are that kind of person. Each of us chooses what kind of person we will become. To become a good person, do the things a good person does. To become a bad person, do the things a bad person does. The opportunity to take action to become the kind of person you want to be is yours.

"I Will Go with You Into the Grave"

In a medieval Christian mystery play, a man asks who will go with him into the grave when he dies and give him support at the Day of Judgment. Time after time, he hears the answer, "I won't go with you into the grave." His wife won't go with him into the grave, his children won't go with him into the grave, his priest won't go with him into the grave, his friends won't go with him into the grave — even his wealth won't go with him into the grave. Finally, the man's good deeds say, "I will go with you into the grave," and the man and his good deeds knock at the door of death, together. Your good deeds will plead for you on the Day of Judgment.

"Do Small Kindnesses for People"

Amy Alkon, aka "The Advice Goddess," does good deeds, and she used to write an advice column for alternative newspapers. She advises, "Do small kindnesses for people." For example, she buys and reads a newspaper every day. When she is finished reading it, she will look around wherever she is — often, she is in a café — and often see somebody who is looking for a newspaper. She will then ask, "Sir, would you like my newspaper?" She points out, "You've noticed a stranger, you've solved their problem, you've gone out of your way to do it, and they're gonna feel very good about that, and I think people will tend to pass on good deeds, do other good deeds, if you do good deeds for them." She adds that "it does make a difference."

"Dear"

One of the things that Kurt Vonnegut, Jr., believes firmly is this: "God d*mn it, you've got to be kind." One of the things that cheers him up is buying a morning cup of coffee in New York City, which he describes as mad for money. He says, "You can go into a little café and the waitress calls you 'dear' even though she knows the bill will be a small expenditure and the tip tiny. So she is responding to you as a person and feels happy and wants to communicate."

Show the Haters that They are Wrong

Robert DeMott and Dave Smith became friends in the early 1970s. They had a number of things in common that facilitated their friendship: they were or would become editors, scholars, teachers, and writers, plus both had been told as undergraduates by professors that they "were not smart enough or able enough to amount to much in the 'real' world" — predictions that they ignored. Mr. DeMott became a noted John Steinbeck scholar, and Mr. Smith became a noted poet.

Cover Photograph for Thomas Middleton's *Women Beware Women*: A Retelling:

https://pixabay.com/photos/portrait-contrast-lighting-woman-4193979/

Educate Yourself
Read Like A Wolf Eats
Be Excellent to Each Other
Books Then, Books Now, Books Forever

***

In this retelling, as in all my retellings, I have tried to make the work of literature accessible to modern readers who may lack some of the knowledge about mythology, religion, and history that the literary work's contemporary audience had.

Do you know a language other than English? If you do, I give you permission to translate this book, copyright your translation, publish or self-publish it, and keep all the royalties for yourself. (Do give me credit, of course, for the original retelling.)

I would like to see my retellings of classic literature used in schools, so I give permission to the country of Finland (and all other countries) to give copies of any or all of my retellings to all students forever. I also give permission to the state of Texas (and all other states) to give copies of any or all of my retellings to all students forever. I also give permission to all teachers to give copies of any or all of my retellings to all students forever. Of course, libraries are welcome to use my eBooks for free.

Teachers need not actually teach my retellings. Teachers are welcome to give students copies of my eBooks as background material. For example, if they are teaching Homer's *Iliad* and *Odyssey*, teachers are welcome to give students copies of my *Virgil's* Aeneid: *A Retelling in Prose* and tell them, "Here's another ancient epic you may want to read in your spare time."

CAST OF CHARACTERS

Duke of Florence.

Lord Cardinal, brother to the Duke.

Two Cardinals more.

A Lord.

Fabritio, father to Isabella.

Hippolito, brother to Fabritio.

Guardiano, uncle to the Foolish Ward.

The Foolish Ward, a rich young heir.

Leantio, a factor, husband to Brancha. A factor is a commercial agent — a merchant's agent or clerk. Leantio's social class was lower than that of Brancha.

Sordido, the Foolish Ward's serving-man.

Livia, sister to Fabritio and Hippolito.

Isabella, daughter to Fabritio.

Brancha, Leantio's wife. A messenger says that she is about sixteen years old.

Mother to Leantio, a widow. She is sixty years old, which this society considers old.

States (aka Nobles) of Florence, Citizens, an Apprentice, Boys, Messenger, and Servants.

SCENE: Florence.

NOTES:

Thomas Middleton's characters tend to be flawed, not saintly.

Some editors say that Livia is the sister of Hippolito, while other editors say that she is the sister-in-law of Hippolito. In 2.2, Livia does call Isabella's mother her sister. The word "sister," however, can mean "sister-in-law." Of course, the words "father" and "brother" can also refer to in-laws. This book assumes that Livia is the sister of Hippolito.

In this society, a person of higher rank would use "thou," "thee," "thine," and "thy" when referring to a person of lower rank. (These terms were also used affectionately and between equals.) A person of lower rank would use "you" and "your" when referring to a person of higher rank.

"Sirrah" was a title used to address someone of a social rank inferior to the speaker. Friends, however, could use it to refer to each other.

The word "wench" at this time was not necessarily negative. It was often used affectionately.

CHAPTER 1

— 1.1 —

Leantio and Brancha met Leantio's mother, and Leantio went over to his mother to speak to her. Leantio and Brancha had recently eloped, and they had just come from Venice to Florence. Brancha was far enough away from Leantio and his mother that she perhaps could not hear them speak about her.

Leantio's mother said to him:

"Thy sight was never yet more precious and happy to me. Welcome with all the affection of a mother that comfort can distill from natural love.

"Since my joy at thy birth — a mother's chief gladness, after she's undergone her curse of sorrows in the pain of childbirth — thou were not dearer to me than this hour that presents thee to my heart.

"Welcome, again!"

Leantio said to himself, "Alas, poor affectionate soul, how her joys speak to me and move me! I have observed it often, and I know it is the fortune commonly of knavish, rebellious children to have the most loving mothers."

He sometimes went against the wishes of his mother, and yet she continued to love him.

Leantio's mother asked him, "Who's this gentlewoman?"

Leantio said:

"Oh, you have named the most highly valuable acquisition that the youth of man had ever knowledge of.

"As often as I look upon that treasure and know that it is mine — there lies the blessing! — it makes me rejoice that I ever was ordained to have a being — an existence — and to live among men."

Leantio was a commercial agent, and he spoke about his wife, Bianca, using terms of commerce.

Leantio continued:

"Life is usually full of fears, and life is usually poor. Let a man truly think about it: to have the toil and griefs of fourscore years put up in a white sheet, tied with two knots."

The white sheet was a shroud, which was tied with knots at the top and the bottom.

Leantio continued:

"I think it should strike earthquakes and put the fear of God in adulterers, when even the very sheets they commit sin in may prove to be, for anything they know, all their last garments.

"Oh, what an example would be there for women then!

"But beauty, which is able to content a conqueror whom the possession of the Earth could scarcely content, keeps me in compass and within limits."

Alexander the Great conquered the world that was known to him, and then he is said to have wept because no more worlds were left for him to conquer.

Leantio continued:

"I find no wish in me inclined sinfully to this man's sister, or to that man's wife. In love's name let them keep their chastity and cleave to their own husbands — it is their duties."

In other words: Brancha's beauty keeps Leantio from wishing to commit adultery.

Leantio continued:

"Now when I go to church, I can pray honestly, nor shall I come like gallants only to see faces, as if lust went to market continually on Sundays."

Some gallants went to church mostly to see the pretty women there.

Leantio continued:

"I must confess I am guilty of one sin, mother, more than the original sin I brought into the world with me."

The original sin was committed in the Garden of Eden. This sin was then passed down to all of Adam and Eve's descendants in the form of an innate tendency to sin.

Leantio continued:

"But that sin I glory in. It is theft, but it is as noble a theft as ever greatness yet shot up with."

It was a theft that could help him rise socially in the world and become a great man.

"What sin is that?" Leantio's mother asked him.

Leantio said:

"It is never to be repented, mother, although sin is death."

Romans 6:23 states, "*For the wages of sin is death* [...]" (King James Version).

Leantio continued:

"I would have died, if I had not sinned, and here's my masterpiece."

He pointed to Brancha and asked:

"Do you now behold her?

"Look on her well, she's mine; look on her better. Now say if it isn't the best piece of theft that ever was committed, and I have my pardon for it.

"It is sealed and ratified from heaven by marriage."

Leantio's mother said, "You are married to her!"

Brancha was a gentlewoman. Leantio was below her in social class.

Leantio said:

"You must keep it secret, mother. I am undone and ruined if you don't keep it secret. If it should become known, then I have lost her. Do just think now what that loss is; life's only a trifle to it!

"From Venice, which is her birthplace, her consent and I have brought her from parents great in wealth, but now greater in rage. But let storms expend their furies; now that we have got a shelter over our quiet innocent loves, we are contented.

"Little money she's brought me. View only her face, and you may see all her dowry, except that which lies locked up in hidden virtues, like jewels kept in cabinets."

Leantio's mother said, "You're to blame — if your obedience to your mother will allow you to hear a check and rebuke — to wrong such a perfection of beauty."

"What!" Leantio said.

Leantio's mother said:

"You have wronged such a creature by drawing her away from her fortune, which, no doubt, in the fullness of time, might have proved rich and noble.

"You don't know what you have done."

Leantio had married Brancha without her parents' permission and therefore he had gotten no dowry. Such a dowry would have allowed her to live the lifestyle to which she was accustomed. If Brancha had stayed at home and had married a man whom her parents approved of, she would have lived and have continued to live a luxurious life.

Leantio's mother continued:

"I during my life can give you but little help, and my death can give you only lesser hopes."

In other words: I can help you only a little while I am alive, and I can leave you little when I am dead.

Leantio's mother continued:

"And hitherto your own means have just barely managed to maintain your life as a single man, and that in hard circumstances, too.

"What ability have you to do her right then in maintenance befitting her birth and virtues?

"Every woman of necessity looks for comfort in life, and most wish to go above and improve on the life to which they were born. They do not wish to be confined by their circumstances, virtues and abilities, bloods, or births, but instead they wish to satisfy their overflowing desires, wishes, and whims."

In other words: Women want to live well and to live better — perhaps much better — than they were raised.

Leantio said quietly to his mother:

"Speak low, sweet mother.

"You are able to spoil and corrupt as many as come within the hearing of what you say. If it is not your fortune to mar everything, I much marvel at it.

"I ask you to not teach her — my wife — to rebel, when she's in a good way to showing obedience to me.

"I ask you to not teach her to rise with other women in commotion and insurrection against their husbands in order to get six gowns a year, and so maintain their cause (when they're once victorious) in all other things that require cost enough.

"They are all of them a kind of spirits soon called up and raised, but not so soon sent down and laid to rest, mother. As, for example, a woman's belly — that is, her appetite or desire for something — is got up in a trice, and it is simply charge — that is, nothing but expense — before her belly is laid down again. So it is always in all their quarrels and in their courses of action.

"And I'm a proud man. I hear nothing about them: nothing about these troublesome spirits. They're very still, I thank my happiness, and they are sound asleep. Please don't let your tongue wake them.

"If you can but rest quietly and be quiet, she will be contented with all conditions that my fortunes bring her to. She will be contented to keep close and live a secluded life at home as a wife who loves her husband. She will be contented to go according to the rate of my ability and live within my means.

"And she will not obey the licentious swinge —the unrestricted sway and impulse — of her own will, like some of her old school fellows.

"She intends to take out and copy other works in a new sampler, and frame the fashion of an honest love, which knows no wants."

Literally, a sampler is a piece of skillful embroidery that can be framed. Brancha will take out — remove — the work of an old sampler and embroider new work in it.

Figuratively, Brancha will follow a way of life different from that of her school friends. They will seek to satisfy their material desires, but Leantio hoped that Brancha will be an obedient wife and live happily within his modest means.

Leantio continued:

"But mocking poverty brings forth more children, to make rich men wonder at divine providence, which feeds mouths of infants, and sends them no infants to feed, but which instead stuffs their rooms with fruitful moneybags and rich possessions and which stuffs their beds with barren wombs."

According to Leantio, one advantage of poverty is that poor people tend to have more children than rich people.

Leantio continued:

"Good mother, don't make things worse than they are because of your too much openness. Please take heed of your too much openness and don't imitate the envy of old people who strive to mar good entertainment because they are past it."

In other words: Old people no longer have sex, and they want to stop the sexual activity of others.

Leantio continued:

"I would have you feel more pity for youth, especially to your own flesh and blood.

"I'll prove to be an excellent husband. Here's my hand."

He held his hand up as if swearing to tell the truth in a court of law.

Leantio continued:

"I will lay in provisions and feed us, I will follow my business roundly, and I will make you a grandmother in forty weeks."

"Roundly" means "energetically," and the word "business" often refers to sex.

Leantio was promising to be a good provider of food and sex for Brancha.

Leantio concluded:

"Go, and please greet her and bid her welcome cheerfully."

Leantio's mother kissed Brancha and said:

"Gentlewoman, thus much is a debt of courtesy, which fashionable strangers pay each other at a kind meeting."

"Then there's more than one kiss. Due to the knowledge I have of your near kinship to me, I am bold to come kiss you again."

Leantio's mother kissed Brancha a second time and said:

"And now I greet you by the name of 'daughter,' which may lay claim to more than ordinary respect."

Leantio's mother kissed Brancha — her daughter-in-law — a third time.

Leantio said to himself, "Why, this is well done now, and I think few mothers of threescore years will improve on it."

Threescore years is sixty years.

"What I can bid you welcome to is humble," Leantio's mother said. "But make it all your own. We are very needy, and we cannot welcome you in accordance with what you're worth."

Leantio said to himself:

"Now this is scurvy; and it is spoken as if a woman lacked her teeth."

The word "scurvy" can mean "annoying," and the disease scurvy can lead to loss of teeth.

Leantio continued saying to himself:

"These old folks talk of nothing but physical defects because they grow so full of them themselves."

Brancha said:

"Kind mother, nothing can be lacking to her who enjoys all her desires. If Heaven will send a quiet peace along with this man's love, then I will be as rich in my mind as virtuous people can be poor in material things.

"This gift of Heaven would make me non-materially rich enough to erect temples of happiness here in my heart and in your home."

In other words: Brancha was saying that she will be satisfied with a contented, happy mind even if she lacks material things.

Brancha continued:

"I have forsaken friends, fortunes, and my country, and hourly I rejoice in it. Here are my friends, and few is the number of good friends."

She then said to Leantio:

"Thy fortunes (however they look, good or bad), I will always name my fortunes. Hopeful or spiteful, they shall all be welcome.

"Whoever invites many guests has guests of all sorts and kinds. He who trades much does drink of all fortunes, yet the fortunes must all be welcome, and treated well, like guests.

"I'll call this place the place of my birth now, and rightly, too; for here my love was born, and that's the birth-day of a woman's joys."

Brancha then said to Leantio:

"You have not bid me welcome since I came."

She was saying that he had not kissed her for a while.

Leantio said, "That I did without question: I did greet you."

"No, surely?" Brancha said. "How was it? I have quite forgotten it."

"It was like this," Leantio said.

He kissed her.

"Oh, sir, it is true," Brancha said. "Now I remember it well. I have done thee wrong. Please take it again, sir."

She kissed him back.

"How many of these wrongs could I endure in an hour and turn over the hour-glass for twice as many more!" Leantio said.

Leantio's mother asked, "Will it please you to walk inside, daughter?"

"Thanks, sweet mother!" Brancha said. "The voice of her who bare me would not be more pleasing."

Leantio's mother and Brancha exited.

Leantio, who worked for a merchant as a factor, said to himself:

"Though my own care — my consciousness and my ambition — and my rich master's trust, lay their commands both on me to practice my career as a factor, this day and night I'll know no other business but her and her dear welcome."

The word "business" can mean "sex" as well as "commercial business."

Leantio continued saying to himself:

"It is a bitterness to think upon tomorrow!

"That I must leave her always to the sweet hopes of the week's end!

"That pleasure should be so restrained and curbed and dependent on the practice of a rich work-master, who never pays until Saturday night!

"By the Virgin Mary, it comes together in a tidy sum then, and it does more good, you'll say."

This day and night Leantio would enjoy Brancha, but the next day he had to go to work for a boss who paid him weekly on Saturday. He would be away from her until he finished working during the week and got paid.

Leantio continued saying to himself:

"Oh, fair-eyed Florence!

"If thou only knew what a most matchless jewel thou now are mistress of, a pride would take thee that would be able to shoot destruction through the bloods of all thy youthful sons."

"Blood" and "pride" can mean "sexual desire." The young men of Florence can be ruined if they fall in love with Brancha.

Leantio continued saying to himself:

"But it is great policy and prudence to keep choice treasures in the obscurest places. Should we show thieves our wealth, it would make them bolder.

"Temptation is a devil that will not hesitate to fasten upon a saint. Take heed of that.

"The jewel — Brancha — is cased up and concealed from all men's eyes. Who could imagine now that a gem were kept of that great value under this plain roof?

"But what about in times when I am absent? What assurance do I have of this restraint and safe-keeping then? Yes! Yes! There's one with her.

"Old mothers know the world; and such as these,

"When sons lock chests, are good to look after keys."

Leantio was worried that other men would see Brancha and pursue her, but he would keep her at home, and he had his mother to watch over her.

Guardiano, Fabritio, and Livia were talking together. Guardiano was the uncle of the Foolish Ward. Fabritio was the father of a woman named Isabella. Livia was the sister of Fabritio and Hippolito.

"What!" Guardiano said. "Has your daughter seen him yet? Do you know that?"

"Him" was Guardiano's Foolish Ward. A ward is a person who is under the care of another person. That person takes care of the ward's affairs. Often, wards are not yet of age to take care of their affairs.

Guardians could benefit financially if they married off a male ward before the ward came of age. The father of the bride would pay the guardian. If the ward declined to marry the woman, his guardian would fine the ward's estate. If the woman declined to marry the ward, the ward's guardian would not financially benefit.

The age of maturity was 21, and readers will learn that the Foolish Ward was almost 20. "Time is calling upon" Guardiano, and he wants to marry off his Foolish Ward.

"It doesn't matter whether she has seen him," Fabritio, the father of the woman whom Guardiano wanted the Foolish Ward to marry, said. "She shall love him."

Guardiano said:

"Nay, let's have fair play. He has been now my ward some fifteen years, and it is my purpose (as time calls upon me, seconded by custom, and such moral virtues) to tender — that is, offer — him a wife.

"Now, sir, this wife I'd eagerly elect out of a daughter of yours. You see my meaning's fair. If now this daughter so tendered (let me use your own word, sir) should undertake to refuse him, I would be hanselled."

A "handsel" is a gift given at the beginning of a year or some other important occasion. Here, it is ironic: "It would be a 'fine' gift, indeed!"

Guardiano said to himself:

"Thus I am obliged to calculate all my words, for the meridian of a foolish old man, to catch his understanding."

The "meridian" is the highest point. Fabritio's intelligence is limited; unfortunately, that is the highest point of his intellectual development.

Guardiano then said out loud:

"What do you answer, sir?"

Fabritio said, "I say still that she shall love him."

"Yet again?" Guardiano said. "And shall she have no reason for this love?"

"Why, do you think that women love with reason?" Fabritio asked.

Guardiano said to himself, "I perceive that fools are not at all hours foolish, no more than wise men are at all times wise."

A proverb stated, "Even a fool sometimes speaks a wise word."

Fabritio then said:

"I had a wife. She ran mad for me; she had no reason for it, for anything I could perceive."

He then asked his sister, Livia:

"What do you think, lady sister?"

Guardiano said to himself:

"That was a fit match, being both out of their wits."

It was a fitting marriage match because both husband and wife were mad in the sense of being insane.

Guardiano then said out loud:

"A loving wife, it seemed that she strove to come as near you as she could."

"Near you" means 1) close to you, and 2) like you, in being mad.

Fabritio replied:

"And if her daughter does not prove mad for love, too, then she does not take after her; nor does she take after me, if she prefers reason before my pleasure."

He then asked Livia, his sister:

"You're an experienced widow, lady sister. Please let your opinion come among us."

Livia said:

"I must offend you then, if truth will do it, and take my niece's part, and call it injustice to force her love to one she never saw.

"Maidens should both see, and like, their possible husband; all that is little enough — it's a small matter.

"If they love truly after that, it is well.

"Considering the length of the marriage commitment, she takes one man in marriage until death. That's a hard task, I tell you; but one may inquire at the end of three years among young wives and see how the game goes."

Fabritio asked, "Why, isn't the man tied to the same observance — the same set of rules — lady sister, and isn't he in one woman?"

Livia said:

"One is enough for him.

"Besides, he tastes of many sundry dishes that we poor female wretches never lay our lips to."

In other words: In marriage, men have more privileges than women. And many men break their marriage vows.

Livia continued:

"These dishes include obedience, indeed, subjection, duty, and such kickshaws [fancy dishes], all of our making, but served to them. And if then sometimes we lick a finger and taste our own cooking, we are not to blame; your best cooks do it."

Hmm. The word "finger" has a sexual meaning.

A proverb stated, "He is an ill cook who cannot lick his own finger."

Fabritio said, "Thou are a sweet lady, sister, and a witty lady."

Livia said:

"A witty lady!

"Oh, the bud of commendation fit for a girl of sixteen!

"I am blown, man — I am in full bloom!"

Livia wanted to be thought wise, not witty.

The word "blown" sometimes also has the connotation of being past the date of best use.

Livia continued:

"I should be wise by this time; and as proof, I have buried my two husbands in good fashion, and I never intend any more to marry."

"No!" Guardiano said. "Why so, lady?"

Livia said:

"Because the third shall never bury me.

"I think I am more than witty.

"What do you think, sir?"

Fabritio said, "I have paid often fees to a counselor who has had a weaker brain."

The counselor may be a lawyer.

Livia said, "Then I must tell you that your money was soon parted from you."

A proverb stated, "A fool and his money are soon parted."

Guardiano said to Fabritio, "Light her now, brother."

In other words: Alight on her now, brother. Answer Livia and bring her down a notch.

And/or, perhaps: Light her up now, brother, and make her angry.

The two men were not literally brothers.

Livia said:

"Where is my niece? Let her be sent for immediately, if you have any hope that it will prove to result in a wedding.

"It is fitting indeed that she should have one sight of him, and reflect upon it, and not be joined in haste, as if they went to stock a newfound land."

Some people leaving Britain to go to Virginia or Newfoundland hastily married before the voyage.

Fabritio said:

"Look out for her uncle, and you're sure to find her.

"Those two are never asunder; they've been heard in discussion at midnight.

"Moonshine nights are noon days with them; they walk out when most people sleep, or rather at those hours, they appear like sleepwalkers, for so they did to me."

He looked up and saw Hippolito and Isabella coming toward them. Hippolito was Isabella's uncle, and Isabella was the woman whom Guardiano and Fabritio wanted to marry Guardiano's Foolish Ward.

Fabritio then said:

"Look, I told you the truth: They're like a chain. Draw but one link, and all the other links follow."

Hippolito and Isabella walked over to them.

Guardiano said:

"Oh, affinity! Oh, kinship! What piece of excellent workmanship are thou!

"Kinship is work that is cleanly wrought, without blemish, for there's no lust, but love in it, and that abundantly. When in stranger things, there is no love at all, except what lust brings."

"Stranger things" is love between people who are not related. According to Guardiano, such love is actually lust.

Fabritio said to Isabella: "Put your mask on! For it is your part to see now, and not to be seen."

Women in Florence at this time customarily wore masks when a suitor was seeing them.

Fabritio continued:

"Bah, make use of your time. See what you intend to like; and I order you, like what you see. Do you hear me? There's no dallying.

"The gentleman's almost twenty, and it is time that he was begetting lawful heirs, and it is time that you were breeding them."

Shocked, Isabella said, "Good father!"

Fabritio said:

"Don't tell me of gossiping tongues and rumors. You'll say the gentleman is somewhat simple-minded.

"Then he is all the better for a husband if you were wise.

"For those who marry fools, live ladies' lives.

"Put the mask on!

"I'll hear no more! He's rich. The fool's hid under bushels."

Livia put the mask on.

Matthew 5:15 states, "*Neither do men light a candle, and put it under a bushel, but on a candlestick; and it giveth light unto all that are in the house*" (King James Version).

The Foolish Ward's foolishness was hidden by his bushels of money.

The Foolish Ward appeared with his back to Livia so that she was viewing his butt.

Livia said, "Not so hid, neither, but for a foul great piece of him, I think. Who will he be when he comes altogether?"

According to Livia, the Foolish Ward already appeared to be foolish, and in the future, he would reveal more foolishness.

The Foolish Ward walked over to them. He was carrying a cat-stick, and Sordido, his serving-man, accompanied him.

The game called Cat was played with two sticks. A short stick with tapered ends that was called the cat was placed on the ground, and a longer stick called the cat-stick was used to hit the cat and send it into the air where the player attempted to hit it again.

The Foolish Ward said to Sordido, "Beat him? I beat him out of the field with his own cat-stick, yet I gave him the first hand."

The first hand is the first turn.

"Oh, strange!" Sordido said.

"I did it," the Foolish Ward said. "Then he set Jacks on me."

A "jack" is a "common fellow." Here, "Jacks" is the name of a tailor.

"What!" Sordido said. "My lady's tailor?"

Tailors had the reputation of being cowards.

"Aye, and I beat him, too," the Foolish Ward said.

"Nay, that's no wonder," Sordido said. "He's used to beating."

"Beaten cloth" was "embroidered cloth." Tailors used to beat gold and silver into cloth and so embroider it, and they were used to being beaten.

"Nay, I tickled him when I came once to my tippings," the Foolish Ward said.

"Tickling" can mean "exciting (someone) sexually."

According to the *Oxford English Dictionary*, "Tipping" is "The action of furnishing or fitting with a tip."

A penis has a tip.

According to the *Oxford English Dictionary*, the verb "tip" can mean "To strike or hit smartly but lightly; to give a slight blow, knock, or touch to [...]."

The word "tippings" can therefore mean "blows."

The Foolish Ward was also talking about the game of Cat.

Sordido said, "Now you talk about your tippings, there was a poulterer's wife who made a great complaint about you last night to your guardianer. She complained that you struck a bump in her child's head as big as an egg."

The guardianer is the Foolish Ward's guardian: Guardiano.

The Foolish Ward said:

"An egg may prove to become a chicken, and then in time the poulterer's wife will gain by it. "

A poulterer can be a bawd, and a chicken can be a prostitute.

The Foolish Ward continued:

"When I am in game, I am furious."

By "in game," the Foolish Ward meant "while playing the game of Cat," but "in game" can also mean "having sex."

The Foolish Ward continued:

"If my mother's eyes came in my way, I would not lose a fair end: a good result. No, if she were alive, with only one tooth in her head, I would risk the striking out of that.

"I think of nobody when I am in play because I am so earnest."

Noticing Guardiano, the Foolish Ward said:

"God's me! My guardianer!"

"God's me!" is an oath.

The Foolish Ward then said:

"Please, lay up my cat and cat-stick somewhere safe."

"Where, sir? In the chimney corner?" Sordido asked.

"Chimney corner!" the Foolish Ward said.

"Yes, sir," Sordido said. "Cats are always safe in the chimney corner, unless they burn their coats."

Hmm. A "cat" can be a "whore," a "chimney" can be a "vagina," and "burn" is a word associated with venereal disease.

"By the Virgin Mary, that I am afraid of!" the Foolish Ward said.

He was afraid of getting a venereal disease.

"Why, then, I will bestow your cat in the gutter, and there she's safe, I am sure," Sordido said.

The Foolish Ward said:

"If I just live to keep a house and be its master, I'll make thee a great man, if meat and drink can do it."

"A great man" is 1) a VIP, or 2) a fat man.

The Foolish Ward continued:

"I can stoop gallantly and pitch out when I wish. I'm dog at a hole. I marvel that my guardianer does not seek a wife for me."

Hmm. A "stoop-gallant" is a word used for venereal disease, "pitch out" can mean "ejaculation," and a "hole" can mean what you think it means. And if you know what "hole" means, you can guess at what "dog" means.

"To be dog at" means "to be skilled and experienced."

A dog at a hole, however, may mean a dog digging at the hole of a rabbit warren. Since the main warren has two or more entrances/exits, if an enemy would come in through one hole, the rabbits can escape from the other hole or holes.

The Foolish Ward continued:

"I declare I will have a bout of sex with the maids if my guardianer does not find a wife for me, or contract myself at midnight to the larder-woman (scullery maid), in the presence of a fool, and a sack-posset."

A man and woman could say the vows of marriage in front of a witness and be legally contracted to marry, but if the witness were a fool, then the contract would be invalid.

A "fool" is also fruit mixed with cream, and a sack-posset was a medicinal drink made with the white wine called sack.

Guardiano called, "Ward!"

The Foolish Ward said, "I feel myself after any exercise horribly prone. Let me just ride. I'm lusty. A cock-horse, immediately, indeed!"

Hmm, the Foolish Ward was prone — that is, eager — to engage in sex after exercise. He had just been playing the game of Cat. A "cat" can be a whore. A cock-horse is a child's hobby-horse, or an adult's whore. Both can be ridden.

Guardiano called, "Why, ward, I say!"

The Foolish Ward said:

"I'll forswear eating eggs on moonshine nights."

In this society, eggs, like many other foods, were thought to be an aphrodisiac.

The Foolish Ward said:

"There's never an egg I eat, it but turns into a cock in four-and-twenty hours; if my hot blood is not taken down in time, surely it will crow shortly."

Hmm. If the Foolish Ward's cock does not come down prematurely, it will "crow," aka ejaculate.

Guardiano called:

"Do you hear, sir?"

He walked over to the Foolish Ward and said:

"Follow me, I must newly school you."

"School me?" the Foolish Ward said. "I scorn that now; I am past schooling. I am not so base to learn to write and read; I was born to better fortunes in my cradle."

The Foolish Ward could not read and write, or, perhaps, he could not read and write well. He was above learning such "base" skills.

The Foolish Ward, Guardiano, and Sordido exited.

Fabritio said to Isabella, "How do you like him, girl? This is your husband. Like him, or don't like him, wench, you shall have him, and you shall love him."

Livia said to Fabritio:

"Oh, hold on there, brother! Although you are a Justice of the Peace, your warrant cannot be served out of your liberty: the place where you have legal jurisdiction.

"You may compel, out of the power of a father, things entirely harsh to a maiden's flesh and blood, but when you come to love, there the soil alters. You're in another country, where your laws are no more valued than the cacklings of geese in Rome's great capitol."

Livia was wrong if she meant that the Romans set little value on the geese of the Capitoline Hill. The geese on the Capitoline Hill were sacred to Juno, and they cackled one night when the Gauls used a hidden trail, hoping to spring a surprise attack upon the Roman general Marcus Manlius. The Romans heard the geese, and they successfully repelled the Gauls.

Usually, however, the Romans would be used to the cackling of the geese and so would ignore it.

Fabritio said, "Marry him she shall then. Let her agree upon love afterwards."

He exited.

Livia said as he exited:

"You speak now, brother, like an honest mortal who walks upon the earth with a staff — like a pilgrim.

"You were up in the clouds before; you'd command love, and so do most old folks who go without it."

Livia then said to her other brother, Hippolito:

"My best and dearest brother! I could dwell here with you. There is not such another seat on earth, where all good parts — good qualities of mind and body — better express themselves."

"You'll make me blush soon," Hippolito said.

Livia said:

"It is just like saying grace before a feast then, and that most comely; thou are all a feast, and she who has thee, is a most happy guest.

"Please cheer up thy niece with special counsel."

Livia exited, leaving Hippolito and Isabella, uncle and niece, alone.

Hippolito said to himself:

"I wish that it were fitting to speak to Isabella what I want to say to her! But it was not a thing ordained; Heaven has forbidden it. And it is most meet and fitting that I should rather perish than that the divine decree receives the least blemish.

"Feed inward, my sorrows. Make no noise. Consume me silent. Let me be stark dead before the world knows I'm sick.

"You — Heaven — see my honesty. If you befriend me, so let it happen."

Hippolito wanted Heaven's blessing of death before he could act on what the audience will learn are his incestuous feelings for his niece: Isabella.

Isabella said to herself:

"Marry a fool! Can there be greater misery to a woman who means to keep her days true to her husband and sexually know no other man? So virtue wills it.

"Why, how can I obey and honor him, when in doing so I must necessarily commit idolatry?

"A fool is but the image of a man, and that is but ill made as well."

A man is made in the image of God, but a fool is only the image of a man and not the real thing, so a woman who honors a fool is honoring an image and so commits idolatry.

Even though a man is made in the image of God, it is an ill-made image.

Isabella continued saying to herself:

"Oh, the heart-breakings of miserable maidens, where love is forced!

"The best condition is but bad enough: When women have their choices, commonly they do just buy their thralldoms — their slavery — and bring great marriage portions — great dowries — to men to keep themselves — women — in subjection.

"It is as if a fearful prisoner should bribe the keeper to be good to him, yet the prisoner still lies in prison, and is glad of good treatment and a kind look sometimes.

"By Our Lady the Virgin Mary, no misery surmounts a woman's! Men buy their slaves, but women buy their masters.

"Yet honesty and love make all this — marriage — happy, and next to the estate and condition of angels, honesty and love make marriage the most blessed estate and condition."

"Honesty" is "loyalty" and "chastity." A chaste person is someone who either engages in no sex or in only ethical sex, such as sex engaged in by a loving husband and a loving wife.

Isabella continued saying to herself:

"Providence, which has made every poison good for some use, and which has set the four warring elements at peace in man, can make a harmony in things that are most strange to and incompatible with human reason."

The four elements are air, earth, fire, and water.

First, there was chaos, but Providence brought order out of chaos.

Isabella continued saying to herself:

"Oh, but this marriage!"

She then said to her uncle, Hippolito, who looked sad:

"What! Are you sad and dejected, too, uncle? Truly, then there's a whole household down — sad and dejected — together.

"Where shall I go to seek my comfort now when my best friend's distressed? What is it that afflicts you, sir?"

Hippolito said:

"Truly, nothing except one grief that will not leave me, and now it is welcome; every man has something to bring him to his end, and this will serve.

"Join my grief with your father's cruelty to you, and that helps my grief increase."

Isabella said, "Oh, be cheered, sweet uncle! How long has this sadness been upon you? I never spied it. What a dull sight I have! How long have you had it, I ask, sir?"

"Since I first saw you, niece, and left Bologna," Hippolito answered.

Isabella said:

"And could you deal so unkindly with my heart, to keep it shut up so long hidden from my pity?"

"Unkindly" means "unnaturally," and "unlike kin."

Isabella continued:

"Alas! How shall I trust your love hereafter?

"Have we passed through so many discussions, and always missed that topic, the most needful one: your sadness? Have we stayed awake whole nights together in discourses and forgotten the main point?

"We are both to blame. This is an obstinate, willful forgetfulness, and the fault is on both parts. Let's lose no time now.

"Begin, good uncle, you who feel it. What is it? What makes you sad?"

Hippolito replied, "You of all creatures, niece, must never hear about it. It is not a thing ordained for you to know."

"Not I, sir?" Isabella said to her uncle. "All my joys that word cuts off. You made profession — you declared — once that you loved me best. It was only a profession — it was only words!"

Hippolito said, "Yes, I do it — I do love — too truly, and I fear that I shall be blamed for it. Know the worst then: I love thee more dearly than an uncle can."

"Why, so you always said, and I believed it," Isabella said.

Hippolito said to himself:

"So simple and pure is the goodness of her thoughts that they don't understand yet the unhallowed language of a near sinner. I must yet be forced (although I risk blushes and embarrassment) to come nearer: to become more explicit."

He said out loud:

"As a man loves his wife, so I love thee."

Isabella said:

"What's that?

"I thought I heard ill news come toward me, which commonly we understand too soon."

Often, we know that someone bears ill news even before they begin speaking.

Isabella continued:

"So then I'll be over-quick at hearing; I'll anticipate it and so prevent it, although my joys fare the harder."

When Isabella knows that someone is about to speak ill news to her, she will prevent them from speaking. Her joys will fare the harder because she will be expending attention and effort at fending off the hearing of ill news.

Isabella continued:

"You should welcome it."

Her uncle should welcome not being able to tell her that he loves her the way a man loves a wife. He should welcome not being able to sin because she will prevent him from sinning.

Isabella's joys shall also fare the harder because she will stop communicating with her uncle.

Isabella continued:

"This ill news shall never come so near my ear again.

"Farewell, all our friendly solaces and discourses.

"I'll learn to live without you, for your dangers are greater than your comforts.

"What's become of truth in love, if we cannot trust such as you, Hippolito, and when blood, which should be love, is mixed with lust!"

"Blood" can mean 1) family, or 2) sexual passion.

Isabella exited.

Alone, Hippolito said to himself:

"The worst can be but death, and let it come.

"He who lives joyless, every day's his doom."

A person's doom is his or her Day of Judgment.

He exited.

Alone, Leantio, the husband of Brancha, was grieving because he had to leave for five days because of work. He said to himself:

"I think I'm even as dull now at departure, as men observe great gallants the next day after a revel."

A revel is a party; Leantio's own revel was having sex with his wife, Brancha.

Leantio continued saying to himself:

"You shall see them look much the way I look now if you look at them closely. It is even a second hell to part from pleasure, when man has got a smack of it."

"Smack" means 1) taste, and 2) kiss.

Leantio continued saying to himself:

"Many holidays coming together make your poor heads — people — idle a great while after, and the holiday slackness is said to stick fast to the people's finger ends and make them less nimble. Even so does game — sex — in a newly married couple; it spoils all thrift for the time, and indeed lies in bed to invent all the new ways for great expenses."

The "expenses" were sexual. Leantio had been expending much semen.

The expenses were also financial. If he could do what he wanted, Leantio would stay home and have sex with his wife instead of going to work even though he knew that the responsible thing to do was to work to support his family.

Brancha and his mother appeared at a bay-window above.

Leantio continued saying to himself:

"See if she has not gotten on purpose now into the bay-window to look after me. I have no power to go and leave now, even if I should be hanged for staying.

"Farewell, all business! I desire no more than I see yonder: my wife. Let the goods at quay look after themselves."

Ships were loaded and unloaded at a quay.

Leantio continued saying to himself:

"Why should I toil my youth out? It is but begging two or three years sooner than I would otherwise beg, and I would stay with her continually. Is it agreed? Should I do this?

"Bah! What a religion have I leaped into?"

His "religion" was sex, which he was valuing more than money.

The word "leap" can mean "have sex."

Leantio continued saying to himself:

"Get out again for shame; the man loves best when his care's most; that shows his zeal to love."

In other words: A man loves best when he takes care to provide for his wife.

Leantio continued saying to himself:

"Foolish fondness is just the idiot to real affection; it is an idiot that plays at hot-cockles with rich merchants' wives."

"Fondness" is a foolish infatuation that plays the "fool" or "jester" to true love, which is the "king" of love.

"Hot-cockles" is a game similar to Blind Man's Bluff, and it is a sexual reference.

Foolish infatuations titillate the wives of rich merchants.

Leantio continued saying to himself:

"It is good to make sport — play and have sex — when the money chest's full, and the long warehouse cracks and bursts open because it is so full.

"But now it is the time of day for us to be wiser. It is early with us; and if they lose the morning of their affairs, they commonly lose the best part of the day."

A proverb stated, "He who sleeps all the morning may go begging all the day after."

Leantio continued saying to himself:

"Those who are wealthy, and have acquired enough, it is after sunset with them. They may rest, grow fat with ease, banquet, and toy, and play and have sex, when such as I enter the heat of the day, and I'll do it cheerfully."

Brancha said, "I perceive, sir, that you're not gone yet. I have good hope you'll stay home now."

"Farewell," Leantio said. "I must not."

"Come, come, please return!" Brancha said. "Tomorrow (adding but a little care more) will dispatch all as well. Believe me it will, sir."

In other words: Take the day off. With a little more effort, you can catch up tomorrow on what you failed to do today.

Leantio said:

"I could well wish myself here where you would have me. But love that's wanton and excessive must be ruled awhile by love that's careful, or all goes to ruin.

"As fitting is a government in love, as it is fitting in a kingdom."

In love and in a kingdom, order is necessary.

Leantio continued:

"Where it is all only lust, it is like an insurrection in the people, which, raised in self-will, wars against all reason.

"But love, which is respective for increase, is like a good king who keeps all in peace."

"Respective for increase" means 1) concerned to have children, and 2) concerned to make a profit.

Much of Leantio's vocabulary consisted of words with both a sexual and a financial meaning.

Leantio continued:

"Once more, farewell."

"Just this one night, I request of you," Brancha said.

Leantio said:

"Alas, I'm in for twenty nights if I stay, and then for forty nights. I have such luck to flesh that I never bought a horse, but he bore double."

Leantio claimed to be lucky in flesh: lucky in bedding female flesh.

The horses he bought were strong enough to bear two riders at the same time.

Any married woman who committed adultery would also bear double: She would bear in bed the weight of her husband and of her lover.

Playwrights in this society often used the word "horse" to pun on "whore."

Leantio continued:

"If I stay any longer, I shall turn an everlasting spendthrift; as you love to be maintained well, do not call me again, for then I shall not care which end goes forward."

"I shall not care which end goes forward" means "I shall not care what happens."

One end that can go forward is the end of a penis.

Leantio concluded:

"Again, I say farewell to thee."

He exited.

Brancha said as he exited, "Since it must happen, farewell, too."

Leantio's mother said:

"Indeed, daughter, you're to blame. You take the course of action to make him an ill husband, truly you do. And that disease — the disease of idleness — is catching, I can tell you. Aye, and it is soon taken by a young man's blood, and that with little urging."

A young man's "blood," aka "sexual passion," would use that idle time to go to bed with his wife.

Brancha began to cry.

Leantio's mother continued:

"Bah, see now, what cause do you have to weep? I wish I had no more cause to weep than you have. I have lived threescore years; if you were as old as I am, then you would have reason to weep, if you thought about it correctly; trust me, you're to blame.

"His absence cannot last five days at most.

"Why should those tears be fetched forth? Can't love even be as well expressed in a good, happy look, but instead it — love — must see her face always in a fountain?"

Brancha's tears were like a fountain.

Leantio's mother continued:

"It shows like a country maid fixing her hair by using a dish of still water as a mirror."

A love-struck maiden would often look at herself in a mirror or look at her reflection in a pool of water to ensure she looked pretty to attract the man she loved.

Leantio's mother continued:

"Come, it is an old custom to weep for love."

She accepted that yes, Brancha's tears had a justification.

Two or three boys, and a citizen or two, along with an apprentice, entered the scene.

The boys said, "Now they come! Now they come!"

"The Duke is coming," the second boy said.

"The nobles are coming," the third boy said.

"How near are they, boy?" a citizen asked.

"In the next street, sir, near at hand," the first boy said.

"You, sirrah, get a stand for your mistress, the best in all the city," the citizen said.

A stand is 1) a place to stand and see the Duke and nobles, and 2) an erection.

The apprentice said, "I have it for her, sir. It was a thing I provided for her overnight. It is ready at her pleasure."

A "thing" can be a penis.

"It is ready at her pleasure." Hmm. "It" is "the stand." Which kind of stand? Both?

"Fetch her to it then," the citizen said. "Away, sir! Go!"

The apprentice exited.

"What's the meaning of this hurry? Can you tell me, mother?" Brancha asked.

Leantio's mother said:

"What a memory I have! I see by that — my forgetfulness — that the years come upon me, and I have grown old.

"Why, it is a yearly custom and festival, religiously observed by the Duke and nobles in a procession to St. Mark's temple, the fifteenth of April."

The festival is the Feast of St. Mark's.

Leantio's mother continued:

"See if my dull brains had not quite forgotten it!

"It was happily questioned of thee — it's a good thing you asked about this — because I would have gone downstairs otherwise and sat like a drone — an idle person — below, and never thought about it.

"I would not wish to be ten years younger again if that meant you would lose seeing this sight! Now you shall see our Duke, who is a goodly gentleman of his years."

"Is he old, then?" Brancha asked.

"About some fifty-five years old," Leantio's mother answered.

"That's no great age in a man," Brancha said. "He's then at his best for wisdom and for judgment."

Leantio's mother said, "The Lord Cardinal, his noble brother, is a comely and handsome gentleman, and he is greater in devotion than in blood."

"Blood" can mean sexual passion.

"He's worthy to be closely noticed," Brancha said.

"You shall behold all our chief nobles of Florence," Leantio's mother said. "You came fortunately in time for this solemn day."

"I hope so always," Brancha said.

Music sounded.

"I hear them near us now," Leantio's mother said. "Do you stand comfortably?"

"Exceedingly well, good mother," Brancha said.

"Take this stool," Leantio's mother said.

"I don't need it," Brancha said, "but I thank you."

"Use your will then," Leantio's mother said. "Do what you want."

In great ceremoniousness arrived bare-headed six knights, then two cardinals, then the Lord Cardinal, and then the Duke, and after him the nobles of Florence by two and two, while a variety of music and song sounded.

They passed by Brancha and Leantio's mother, who watched from a window, and then they exited.

"How do you like it, daughter?" Leantio's mother asked.

Brancha said:

"It is a noble state! I think my soul could dwell upon the dignity of such a solemn and most worthy custom.

"Didn't the Duke look up? I thought he saw us."

Leantio's mother said, "That's everyone's idea who sees a Duke. If he looks steadfastly, everyone thinks that he looks straight at them, when he, perhaps, that good, careful, responsible gentleman, never pays attention to anyone, but the look he casts is at his own intentions, and his object is only the public good."

"That is most likely so," Brancha said.

Leantio's mother, "Come, come, we'll end this discussion downstairs."

They exited.

CHAPTER 2
— 2.1 —

Hippolito and his sister — the widow Lady Livia — talked together. He had told her that he loved Isabella, their niece.

"This is a strange affection, brother!" Livia said. "When I think about it, I wonder how thou came by it."

"Even as easily as man comes by destruction, which often he wears in his own bosom," Hippolito said.

Livia asked:

"Is the world so populous in women, and is creation so prodigal in beauty, and so various, and yet does love turn thy point to thine own blood — thine own kin?"

"Point" means 1) the pointing of the tip of a compass needle, and 2) the pointing of the tip of a penis.

Despite the large number of beautiful women in the world, Hippolito was sexually desiring a close relative: Isabella, his niece.

Livia then said:

"It is somewhat too unkindly."

"Unkindly" means "unnaturally," and "unlike kin."

Livia continued:

"Must thy eye dwell evilly on the fairness of thy kindred, and not seek where it should? Thy eye is confined now in a narrower prison than was made for it. Thy eye is allowed a stranger."

In other words: Sexual love is permitted between people who are not closely related to each other. Therefore, cast your eye upon a stranger: someone who is not related to you.

Livia continued:

"And where bounty — that is, generosity — is made the great man's honor, it is ill husbandry to spare and to be frugal, and servants shall have small thanks for it."

In other words: When a man gets honor by being generous, he ought not to be frugal, and he will not thank his servants if they are frugal.

Also in other words: You, Hippolito, should love many women.

Livia continued:

"So he who spares free means and spends of his own stock seems to scorn and mock Heaven's bounty."

In other words: Lots of women were around for Hippolito to love and have sex with. By rejecting them and instead pursuing his own stock, aka kin, aka Isabella, he was rejecting Heaven's bounty.

When applied to sex, a man ought to freely spend, or expend — ejaculate — but not with his own niece.

Hippolito said, "Never was a man's misery so soon and so well summed up, recounting how truly I behave."

Livia said:

"I love you so much that I shall risk much to keep from you a change as fearful as this grief will bring upon you."

She was saying that she wanted to spare him grief. For him not to love Isabella would cause him much grief.

Livia continued:

"Indeed, it even kills me when I see you faint under a reprimand, and I'll stop reprimanding you, although I know nothing can be better for you.

"Please, sweet brother, let not passion and suffering waste the goodness of thy time, and of thy fortune.

"Thou must keep and guard the treasure of that life — your life — I love as dearly as my own; and if you think that my former words are too bitter (which were ministered by truth and zeal), it is but a hazarding of grace and virtue."

"A hazarding of grace and virtue" means "risking the loss of a state of Christian grace and virtue" — that is, "risking damnation."

"Grace and virtue" also apply to Isabella, who has both qualities. So does Brancha, Leantio's wife.

Readers will find out that Livia is willing to put Isabella's grace and virtue and Leantio's wife's grace and virtue at risk.

Livia would also hazard whatever grace and virtue she had to get Hippolito what he wanted.

Livia continued:

"And I can bring forth as pleasant fruits as sensuality wishes in all her teeming, fertile longings. This I can do."

Livia was saying that she could satisfy men's sensuality. One way to do that would be to have sex with them. Another way would be to provide them with a lover.

Hippolito said, "Oh, nothing that can make my wishes perfect and completed!"

Hippolito was saying that Livia could not offer him what he most desired: Isabella.

Livia said:

"I wish that your love was pawned to it, brother, and as soon lost that way, as I could win."

"That your love was pawned to it" meant "that you bet your love on the outcome."

Livia was saying that she could get Isabella for Hippolito, and she was saying that she wished Hippolito could lose his love for Isabella as easily as she could get Isabella for him.

Livia continued:

"Sir, I could give as shrewd and cunning an attack against chastity, as any she who wears a tongue and gossips in Florence. She'd need to be a good horsewoman, and sit fast, whom my strong argument could not unseat at last."

According to Livia, she can offer reasons against chastity that would defeat even the best reasons for chastity.

"Chastity" is 1) no sex, or 2) only ethical sex, such as that between a loving husband and a loving wife.

Livia continued:

"Please take courage, man; although I should advise another man to despair, yet I am full of pity concerning thy afflictions, and I will venture strenuously — I will not name for what because it is not handsome and decent.

"When you see the outcome of what I say, praise me."

"Then I am afraid that I shall not praise you quickly," Hippolito said.

He believed that it would take time for her to succeed in her objective, which was not handsome and decent.

Readers can guess that she wanted to get Isabella for Hippolito.

Livia said:

"This is the comfort: You are not the first, brother, who has attempted things more forbidden than this seems to be."

This sentence made three points:

1) Hippolito has attempted things more forbidden than this: sleeping with his niece.

2) Other people have previously attempted things more forbidden than this: incest.

3) This — incest — *seems* to be forbidden.

Livia continued:

"I'll minister all cordials — medicinal drinks — now to you because I'll cheer you up, sir."

"I am past hope," Hippolito said.

Livia said:

"Love, thou shall see me do a strange cure then, as ever was wrought on a disease so mortal and deadly, and so near akin to shame.

"When shall you see her?"

"Never more in comfort," Hippolito answered.

"You're so impatient, too," Livia said.

"Will you believe me?" Hippolito said. "By God's death, she's forsworn my company, and sealed and confirmed it with a blush."

Livia said:

"So, I perceive that all lies upon my hands then; well, all the more glory when the work's finished."

A servant entered the scene.

Livia asked the servant:

"How are things now, sir? What is the news?"

"Madam, your niece, the virtuous Isabella, has alighted from her coach just now in order to see you," the servant said.

Livia said to Hippolito:

"That's great fortune — very good luck. Sir, your stars bless you."

She then said to the servant, who was waiting for orders:

"Fool! Lead her in."

The servant exited.

"What's this to me?" Hippolito asked.

He was asking, What does this mean for me?

Livia interpreted his sentence in this way: What does this require from me?

"Your absence, gentle brother," Livia said. "I must bestir my wits for you."

"Aye, to great purpose," Hippolito said.

He exited.

Livia said:

"Curse you! I wish that I did not love you so well!

"I'll go to bed, and leave this deed undone.

"I am the fondest and the most foolish where I once feel affection and love. I am the fullest of cares when it comes to their healths, and when it comes to their ease. Indeed, I do that so much that I look always only slenderly and negligently when it comes to my own health.

"I take a course of action to pity him so much now that I have no pity left for modesty and myself.

"This is what it is to grow so liberal and over-generous; you will find few sisters who love their brother's case above their own honesties."

She loved Hippolito, her brother, and she would attempt to help him sleep with Isabella, their niece.

Livia continued:

"But if you question my affections, that will be found my fault."

Her fault is figuratively her vulva. Literally, one meaning of "fault" is "crack."

Isabella entered the scene.

Livia said to her:

"Niece, your love's welcome.

"Alas, what draws that paleness to thy cheeks? This approaching forced marriage to the ward?"

Isabella said, "It helps make me pale, good aunt, among some other griefs, but those I'll keep locked up in modest silence, for they are sorrows that would shame the tongue, more than they grieve the thought."

"Indeed, the ward is simple," Livia said.

Someone who is "simple" is a fool.

Isabella said:

"Simple!

"That would be all right. Why, one might make good shift — might succeed — with such a husband.

"But he's a congenital fool entailed by heredity; he halts downright in it. He stops completely at 'fool' and will never improve."

Livia said, "And knowing this, I hope it is at your choice to take or refuse him as your husband, niece."

"You know that it is not my choice," Isabella said. "I loathe him more than beauty can hate death, or hate age, death's spiteful neighbor."

"Let your loathing appear then," Livia said.

"How can I, being born with that obedience, which must submit under a father's will?" Isabella said. "If my father commands, I must necessarily consent."

"Alas, poor soul!" Livia said. "Don't be offended, please, if I set aside the name of 'niece' awhile and bring in pity in a stranger fashion. Information lies here in this breast that would cross and thwart this marriage match."

"What! Cross and thwart it, aunt?" Isabella said.

"Aye, and give thee more liberty and license than thou have reason yet to apprehend and understand," Livia said.

The word "license" includes "sexual license."

"Sweet aunt, in goodness do not keep hidden from me what may befriend my life," Isabella said.

Livia said:

"Yes, yes, I must when I return to reputation, and think upon the solemn vow I made to your dead mother, my most loving sister."

Isabella's dead mother must be Livia's sister-in-law because Fabritio is Isabella's father, and he is also Livia's brother.

Livia continued:

"As long as I have her memory between my eyelids and in my mind, look for no pity now."

"Look for no pity now" means "look for no information now."

Isabella began, "Kind, sweet, dear aunt —"

Livia interrupted, "No, it was a secret that I have taken special care of, delivered by your mother on her deathbed. That's nine years ago now, and I'll not part from it yet, although there never was a fitter time than now, nor a greater cause for revealing it."

Isabella began, "As you desire the praises of a virgin —"

Livia interrupted, "Good sorrow! I would do thee any kindness if I could do it without wronging secrecy or reputation."

"Neither of which (as I have hope of fruitfulness and having children) shall receive wrong from me," Isabella said.

"Nay, it would be your own wrong, as much as any's, should it ever come to that," Livia said.

"I need no better means to work persuasion then," Isabella said.

Livia said:

"Let it suffice that you may refuse this fool, or you may take him, as you see occasion for your advantage; the best wits will do it.

"You've liberty enough in your own will. You cannot be forced to accept the fool as your husband. The flower grows (if you could pick it out) that makes whole life sweet to you.

"That which you call your father's command is nothing — it is of no consequence. So then your obedience must necessarily be as little.

"If you can make an effort here to taste your happiness, or pick out anyone who pleases you, it may do you much good."

"Taste your happiness" may be innuendo about oral sex.

Livia continued:

"You see your cheer. I'll make you no set dinner."

"Cheer" means 1) gladness, and 2) food.

Livia was giving Isabella partial information, not a full and satisfying "dinner."

"And trust me, I may starve for all the good I can find yet in this," Isabella said. "Sweet aunt, deal more plainly with me. Speak clearly and openly."

"Tell me whether I should trust you now if you were to swear an oath to keep the information secret, and if I were to tell you a secret that would startle you, how will I be sure of you in faith and in silence?" Livia asked.

"Equal assurance may I find in God's mercy on the Day of Judgment, as you may find for that in me," Isabella answered.

"It shall suffice," Livia said. "Then know, however custom has made good and approved for reputation's sake, the names of 'niece' and 'aunt,' between you and me, we're nothing less."

In other words: They are not aunt and niece; they are not biologically related.

According to the *Oxford English Dictionary*, an obsolete meaning of "nothing less" is "*Anything rather than the thing in question. Often used to express denial: far from it.*"

"How's that?" Isabella asked.

Livia said:

"I told you I should start your blood."

"Start" can mean "startle," and "start your blood" can mean "arouse your sexual passion."

Livia continued:

"You are no more allied to any of us (except what the courtesy of opinion casts upon your mother's memory, and your name) than the most complete stranger is —"

In other words: People believed that Isabella's mother was chaste and faithful to her husband, and so they believed that Isabella was legitimate.

Livia continued:

"— or one begotten at Naples when the husband resides at Rome. There's so much odds between us: There is much distance in our relationship. Since your knowledge wished more instruction, and I have your oath in pledge for silence, it makes me talk the more freely.

"Didn't the report of that famed Spaniard, the Marquis of Coria, since your time was ripe for understanding and you became an adult, ever fill your ears with wonder?"

"Yes," Isabella said. "What about him? I have heard his deeds of honor often related when we lived in Naples."

"You heard the praises of your father then," Livia said.

"My father!" Isabella said.

Livia was leading Isabella to believe that the Marquis of Coria was her father, the result of an affair between him and her mother in Naples while her reputed father, Fabritio, was in Rome on business. If that were true, then Hippolito would not be her blood relative. And if that were true, then a sexual relationship between Isabella and Hippolito would not be incestuous.

Livia said:

"That was he, your father, but all the business — the sex affair — was so carefully and so discreetly carried out that reputation received no spot by it — not a blemish.

"Your mother was so wary until her death that no one knew it except her conscience and her friend — that is, her lover — until her penitent confession made it my knowledge, and now because of my pity for you, it is your knowledge. If not for my pity for you, this knowledge would have been a long time coming to you.

"And I hope care and love alike in you, made good by oath, will see it take no wrong now.

"How weak are the commands now of whom you call father.

"How vain are all his enforcements and your obedience!

"And what a largeness — an opportunity — you have in your will and liberty, to take, or to reject, or to do both."

The word "do" can mean "have sex with."

"Will and liberty" means "self-determination and freedom," including in sexual matters.

Livia was saying that Isabella could sexually have the Foolish Ward, or Hippolito, or neither, or both.

Since the Foolish Ward would soon come into wealth, Isabella could marry him for his money while having an affair with Hippolito. Marriage to the Foolish Ward could also serve to hide an affair by Isabella with Hippolito.

Livia continued:

"For fools will serve to father wise men's children: They will raise other men's children and pay the costs of doing so.

"All this you have time to think about.

"Oh, my wench! Nothing overthrows our sex but indiscretion."

In other words: As long as women are discreet, they can do what they want.

Livia continued:

"If not for our indiscretion, we might otherwise do as well as any brittle — frail — people under the great canopy of the sky.

"I ask that you don't forget just to call me aunt still. Take heed of that; it may be noticed in time if you don't.

"But keep your thoughts to yourself, from all the world, from kindred, and from your dearest friend; indeed, I entreat you, keep your thoughts from him whom all this while you have called uncle.

"And although you love him dearly, as I know that his merits claim as much even from a stranger, yet do not let him know this secret; please do not. As ever thou have hope of additional pity and assistance from me, if thou should stand in need of it, do not do it."

"Believe my oath," Isabella said. "I will not."

Livia said:

"Why, well said."

She then said to herself:

"Whoever shows more craft and trickery to undo and ruin a maidenhead, I'll resign my part to her."

Everything that she said to Isabella about Fabritio not being her father was a lie.

As Livia exited, Hippolito entered the scene.

Livia went to him and whispered, "She's thine own; go to her."

Livia finished her exit.

Hippolito said, "Alas, fair flattery — pretty words — cannot cure my sorrows!"

Isabella said to herself:

"Have I passed so much time in ignorance and never had the means to know myself until this blessed hour?"

Actually, Isabella did not now know herself. Livia, her aunt, had lied to her about who Isabella's father is.

Isabella continued saying to herself:

"I give thanks to Livia's virtuous pity that brought it now to light.

"I wish that I had known it just one day sooner. Hippolito would then have received in favors — tokens of love — what (poor gentleman) he took in bitter words: a slight and harsh reward for one of his deserts."

Hippolito said to himself, "There seems to me now more anger and distraction in her looks. I'm going: I'll not endure a second storm. The memory of the first has not passed yet."

Isabella said to herself, "Have you returned, you comforts of my life? In this man's presence, I will keep you fast now, and I will sooner part eternally from the world than I will part from my good joys in you."

She said out loud to Hippolito:

"Please forgive me. I did but chide and rebuke you in jest. The best loves do it sometimes; it sets an edge upon affection — it gives love a sharper relish.

"When we invite our best friends to a feast, it is not all sweetmeats that we set before them. There's something sharp and salty, both to whet the appetite, and to make them taste their wine well.

"So, I think, after a friendly, sharp, and savory chiding and clash, a kiss tastes wondrously well, and full of the grape.

"What do thou think, doesn't a kiss taste wondrously well?"

She kissed him.

Hippolito said, "It is so excellent that I don't know how to praise it, what to say to it."

Isabella said, "This marriage shall go forward."

"With the ward?" Hippolito asked. "Are you in earnest?"

"It would be ill for us otherwise," Isabella said.

Hippolito said to himself, "For *us*! What does she mean by that?"

Isabella said to herself:

"Truly, I begin to be so well, I think, within this hour, despite all this marriage match with the ward, a match that is able to kill one's heart, that nothing can pull me down now.

"If my 'father' — Fabritio — were to provide a worse fool yet (which I should think would be a hard thing to achieve) for me to marry, I'd have him instead of this ward.

"The worse the fool, the better. No fool can come amiss now if he lacks intelligence enough."

The stupider her husband was, the more easily she could manipulate him.

Isabella continued saying to herself:

"As long as discretion, merit, and judgment love me, I have sufficient contentment and happiness!"

Isabella believed that Hippolito's qualities included discretion, merit, and judgment.

Isabella then said to Hippolito:

"She who comes once to be a wife with her own house to keep, must not look every day to fare and eat well, sir, like a young virginal waiting-gentlewoman in service.

"For the waiting-gentlewoman feeds customarily as her lady does. No good bit passes her, but the waiting-gentlewoman gets a taste of it.

"But when she comes to keep house for herself, she's glad of some choice cates — choice delicacies — then once a week, or twice at most, and she is glad if she can get them. So must affection learn to fare with thankfulness.

"Please make your love no stranger, sir, that's all."

When Isabella becomes the wife of the Foolish Ward, her opportunities to have sex with Hippolito will be limited: They will be occasional, not daily, delights.

Isabella then said to herself:

"Although you are one — a stranger — yourself, and don't know it, and I have sworn you must not."

Isabella believed that Hippolito was a stranger to her — that is, she believed that he was not a blood relative to her.

She exited.

Alone, Hippolito said to himself:

"This is beyond me. Never have joys come so unexpectedly to meet desires in man!

"How did she come to be like this? What has Livia done to her? Can anyone tell me?

"This is beyond sorcery, drugs, or love-powders.

"Surely, this must be the result of some art that has no name — some art strange to me despite all the wonders I ever met with throughout my ten years of travels, but I'm thankful for it.

"This marriage now must necessarily go forward. It is the only veil wit and intelligence can devise to keep our acts hidden from sin-piercing eyes."

If Isabella were married to the Foolish Ward, the marriage would provide some cover for their adulterous and incestuous affair.

Somewhat related: In past times, some gay movie stars would marry a woman as a way to keep the movie-going public from learning that the movie stars were gay.

In Livia's house, Guardiano and Livia entered a room in which a chess board was set out.

Livia said, "What, sir! A gentlewoman so young, so fair, as you described, spied standing at the widow's window?"

"She!" Guardiano said.

"Our Sunday-dinner woman?" Livia asked.

Guardiano said:

"And Thursday supper-woman. The same widow still."

Leantio's mother may have been fed twice a week as an act of charity.

Guardiano continued:

"I don't know how she came by her, but I'll swear that she's the prime gallant woman for a face in Florence, and no doubt other parts follow their leader: her face."

Those other parts include the private parts.

Guardiano continued:

"The Duke himself first spied her at the window; then in a rapture, as if admiration would be poor when it was single and unshared, beckoned me, and pointed to the wonder warily, as one who feared she would withdraw her splendor too soon, if too much gazed at.

"I never knew him to be so infinitely taken with a woman, nor can I blame his appetite, or accuse his raptures and passion of being only a slight folly.

"She's a creature who is able to draw a noble away from serious business and make it their best piece — their best accomplishment, aka masterpiece — to do her service."

"Do" can mean "have sex," and "service" can mean "sexual service."

In other words: The noble's best achievement in his life would be to have sex with this woman.

Guardiano continued:

"What course of action shall we devise? He has spoken twice about her now."

"Twice?" Livia said.

Guardiano said, "It is beyond your apprehension how strangely that one look has caught his heart. It would prove to be worth a huge amount in wealth and favor to those who should give him his peace of mind by satisfying his desires."

Livia said, "And if I don't do it, or at least come as near it (if your art and skill will take a few small pains and second — help — me) as any wench in Florence of my standing, I'll quite give over and shut up shop in cunning."

If she couldn't bring the Duke and the woman, who was Branche, together in an affair, then she would give up and quit dealing in secret assignations.

Guardiano said, "It is for the Duke; and if I fail to help you achieve your purpose, may all means to come by riches or advancement skip over and miss me."

"Let the old woman then be sent for with all speed, and then I'll begin," Livia said.

The old woman was Leantio's mother.

Guardiano said:

"May a good conclusion — success — follow, and a sweet one, after this stale beginning with old ware."

The old woman was metaphorically "old ware."

Guardiano called for a servant:

"Within there!"

A servant entered the room and asked, "Sir, do you call?"

Guardiano said, "Come nearer, and listen to me here."

He whispered to the servant.

Livia said to herself, "I myself long to see this absolute and perfect creature who wins the heart of love, and who wins so much praise."

"Go, sir, make haste," Guardiano said to the servant. "Be quick."

Livia said to the servant:

"Tell the old woman that I request her — the old woman's — company.

"Do you hear me, sir?"

"Yes, madam," the servant said.

He exited.

"That will bring her quickly here," Livia said.

Guardiano said:

"I wish it were done; the Duke waits and longs for the good hour."

The "good hour" will be the hour the Duke seduces — or rapes — Brancha.

Guardiano continued:

"And I wait and long for the good fortune that may spring from it. I have had a lucky hand these fifteen years at such court passage with three dice in a dish."

"Court passage" is a game played with three dice. It is also amorous affairs played at court.

In the slang of this society, "to die" meant "to orgasm."

The singular of "dice" is "die," and "three dice in one dish" may mean "three orgasms in one dish."

A dish is a container that sometimes holds food. A vagina is a container that sometimes holds a penis.

Possibly, the three dice are Guardiano, the Duke, and a pretty woman. Guardiano may have often acted as a pandar for the Duke.

Or the three dice could be Leantio, Guardiano, and the Duke. The dish could be Brancha.

Fabritio entered the scene.

Guardiano greeted him: "Signior Fabritio!"

Fabritio said, "Oh, sir, I bring an alteration in my mouth now."

The alteration was in Isabella's attitude toward marriage with the Foolish Ward, but Guardiano deliberately misunderstood him to be talking about an alteration in his speech: from foolish to wise.

Guardiano said out loud:

"An alteration!"

He then said to himself:

"No wise speech, I hope. He doesn't mean to talk wisely, does he, I trust?"

Guardiano then said out loud:

"Good! What's the change, I ask, sir?"

"A new change," Fabritio said.

Guardiano said, "Another yet! Indeed, there's enough already."

"New change" was wordy. A change is new.

Fabritio said, "My daughter loves him now."

"Whom does she love, sir?" Guardiano asked.

Fabritio said:

"She affects him beyond thought!

"Who but the ward indeed! No talk but of the ward! She would choose him to be her husband above all the men she ever saw!

"My will goes not so fast as her consent now. Her duty always gets before and anticipates my command."

Guardiano said, "Why then, sir, if you'll have me speak my thoughts, I smell — that is, I predict — it will be a marriage match."

"Aye, and a sweet young couple, if I have any judgment," Fabritio said.

Guardiano said to himself about Fabritio's judgment:

"Indeed, that's little."

Guardiano then said out loud:

"Let her be sent for tomorrow, before noon, and handsomely tricked up, aka dressed up; for about that time I mean to bring her in and tender her to him."

"Him" is Guardiano's ward.

Fabritio said, "I promise you that she will be beautiful; I will see that her things are laid ready, everything in order, and I will have some part of her tricked up tonight."

"Why, well said," Guardiano replied.

Fabritio said, "It was a custom her mother had. When she was invited to an early wedding, she'd dress her hair the night before, sponge herself, and give her neck three lathers."

Guardiano said to himself, "Never a halter? No halter?"

A halter for a horse or a cow is made of leather. Halters, aka nooses, for hanging people are made of rope.

Fabritio said, "She'd put on her pearl necklace and her ruby bracelets, and she'd lay ready all her tricks and thingamajigs — trinkets."

"So must your daughter do," Guardiano said.

"I'll set about it immediately, sir," Fabritio said.

He exited.

Livia said, "How he sweats in the foolish zeal of fatherhood at the rate of six ounces an hour — he sweats profusely — and he seems to toil as much as if his cares and concerns were wise ones!"

Guardiano said, "You've let his folly blood — that is, flow — in the right vein, lady."

"Blood" can be a verb meaning "flow." As a verb, "let" can mean "suffer" and "permit."

Bloodletting was believed to be a way of curing some diseases.

The Foolish Ward, however, was sweating, not bleeding, and so his foolishness was not being cured. His blood was still flowing in his veins.

Livia was doing nothing to stop the Foolish Ward from being a fool. She was merely describing his foolishness.

Seeing the Foolish Ward arriving, Livia said:

"And here comes his sweet son-in-law who shall be. They're both allied in wit before the marriage. What will they be hereafter when they are nearer?

"Yet they can go no further than the fool. There's the world's end in both of them: They can go no further."

In other words: Fabritio and the Foolish Ward cannot be more foolish than they already are.

The Foolish Ward and Sordido, his servant, entered the scene. One was carrying a shittlecock, and the other was carrying a battledore.

These implements were a shuttlecock and a racket used in an early version of badminton.

"Now, young heir!" Guardiano said.

"What's the next business after shittlecock, now?" the Foolish Ward asked Sordido.

Guardiano said to the Foolish Ward, "Tomorrow you shall see the gentlewoman who must be your wife."

The Foolish Ward said:

"There's even another thing, too, that must be kept up with a pair of battledores."

"A pair of battledores" are metaphorically "a pair of testicles."

They could keep up a penis that would keep his wife up at night.

The Foolish Ward then said:

"My wife! What can she do?"

In this society, "what" can mean "who," and "do" can mean "have sex with."

Guardiano said, "That's a question you should ask yourself, Ward, when you and your wife are alone together."

The Foolish Ward said:

"That's as I wish."

He wanted to be married.

The Foolish Ward continued:

"A wife's to be asked anywhere, I hope. I'll ask her in a congregation, if I have a mind to it, and so save a license."

By publicly announcing the banns — the intention to marry — the Foolish Ward could avoid the need to purchase a special marriage license; however, "asking [announcing or proclaiming] the banns" is not the same thing as asking a woman to marry you.

The Foolish Ward continued:

"My guardianer has no more wit and intelligence than an herb-woman who sells away all her sweet herbs and nosegays [bouquets] and keeps her stinking breath to blow on her own pottage to cool it."

The Foolish Ward thought that his guardian, Guardiano, was foolish because he was giving the Foolish Ward a beautiful woman in marriage and not providing one for himself.

"Pottage" is porridge, soup, or stew.

Sordido said to his master, the Foolish Ward, "Let me be at the choosing of your beloved, if you desire a woman of good parts."

"Parts" are 1) accomplishments, and 2) body parts.

"Thou shall be at the choosing, sweet Sordido," the Foolish Ward said.

Sordido said:

"I have a plaguey guess: a shrewd and confounded judgment.

"Leave it to me alone to see what she is; if I just look upon her, straightaway I know all her faults to a hair, faults that you may refuse her for."

A "fault" can be a vulva, and the hair may be a pubic hair.

The Foolish Ward said, "Do thou know all those faults? I ask thee please to let me hear them, Sordido."

Sordido said:

"Well, listen to them closely then. I have them all in rhyme:

"The wife your guardianer ought to tender,

"Should be pretty, straight, and slender;

"Her hair not short, her foot not long,

"Her hand not huge, nor too, too loud her tongue.

"No pearl in eye, nor ruby in her nose."

In other words: no cataract (or other white spot) or red nose due to pimples or alcoholism.

Sordido continued:

"No burn or cut, except what the catalogue shows."

Burning is associated with venereal disease.

The catalogue of desirable things to look for in a woman includes one kind of cut: That kind of "cut" is a vulva.

Sordido continued:

"She must have teeth, and those no black ones,

"And kiss most sweet when she does smack once.

"Her skin must be both white and plump;

"Her body straight, not hopper-rumped.

Or wriggle sideways like a crab."

A hopper-rump is large like a hopper: a machine into which corn is poured so it can be ground. The hopper makes a shaking movement.

Oddly, Sordido's catalogue of desirable things to look for in a woman does not include big butts that wiggle.

Some people think that Sir Mix-a-Lot's "Baby Got Back," aka "I Like Big Butts," is a novelty song. It's not. The man is just telling it like it is.

Sordido continued:

"She must be neither slut nor drab [whore],

"Nor go too splay-foot with her shoes.

"To make her smock [petticoat] lick up the dews."

A person with splayed feet has feet that are turned outward while walking.

Sordido continued:

"And two things more, which I forgot to tell ye,

"She must have bump in neither back nor belly."

In other words: She must not be humpbacked or pregnant.

Sordido concluded:

"These are the faults that will not make her pass.

The Foolish Ward said, "And if I don't spy these, I am a rank ass."

Sordido said, "Nay, more; by right, sir, you should see her naked, for that's the ancient order."

King Henry VIII's Lord Chancellor, Thomas More, had some novel ideas that he wrote about in his book *Utopia*. For example, he thought that couples about to be married should see each other naked. In real life, when a lawyer called on him and asked to be married to Megg (Thomas More's daughter), Thomas More took him to her bedroom, where she was asleep, and then he swept the bedcovers back and her nightgown up. Rudely awakened, Megg immediately turned over on her stomach. The delighted lawyer said, "I have seen both sides," and then he patted her butt and said, "Thou art mine."

The Foolish Ward said:

"See her naked? That would be good sport, indeed. I'll have the books turned over and examined, and if I discover in the written record that it is the custom for her to be seen naked before marriage, she shall not have a rag on.

"But wait, wait! What if she should desire to see me naked, too?

"I would be in a 'sweet' case then."

The word "case" means 1) situation, or 2) covering (clothing, or skin).

The word "case" can also mean "vagina."

The Foolish Ward concluded:

"I have such a foul skin."

Sordido said, "But you have a clean shirt, and that makes amends, sir."

According to rock band ZZ Top, "Every girl crazy 'bout a sharp-dressed man."

The Foolish Ward said, "I will not see her naked for that trick — my being naked, too — though."

He exited.

Sordido said after him:

"Then take her with all faults with her clothes on! Women may hide a number of faults with a bum-roll."

A bum-roll is a cushion that women wore around their hips. Over the cushion, the women's skirts were arranged.

Sordido then said to you, the readers:

"Truly, the choosing of a wench in a huge farthingale is like the buying of ware under a great penthouse."

A farthingale is a hooped skirt. Bum-rolls and farthingales hid the bottom part of a woman's body.

A penthouse was a sloping roof attached to an outside wall of a shop. It would protect the shop's door and window, but it also would make the shop dark so shoddy goods were more difficult to examine closely.

Sordido continued saying to you, the readers:

"What with the deceit of one, and the deceptive light of the other, mark my speeches, he may have a diseased wench in his bed, and rotten stuff in his breeches."

"Rotten stuff" can be 1) shoddy cloth, or 2) venereal disease.

Sordido exited.

Guardiano said to Livia, "The marriage may succeed handsomely."

"I see small hindrance," Livia said.

A servant walked into the room. Leantio's mother followed him.

Livia said to the servant, "How are things now? So soon returned?

Referring to Leantio's mother, Guardiano said, "She has come."

Livia said:

"That's well.

"Widow, come, come, I have a great quarrel with you. Indeed, I must chide you in that you must be sent for. You make yourself so much a stranger and never come to visit us, and yet you are so near a neighbor, and so unkind.

"Truly, you're to blame; you cannot be more welcome to any house in Florence, that I'll tell you."

Leantio's mother said, "My thanks must necessarily acknowledge so much, madam."

Livia said:

"How can you be so much a stranger then?

"I sit here sometimes whole days together without company, when business draws this gentleman away from home."

Guardiano spent much time with Livia, and he and the Foolish Ward lived in her house.

Livia continued:

"And I should be happy in company, which I so well enjoy, such as that of yours.

"I know you're alone, too; so why shouldn't we, like two kind neighbors, then, supply the needs of one another, having tongue-discourse and the gift of gab, experience in the world, and such kind helps to laugh down time, and meet age merrily?"

Leantio's mother said, "You are joking about age, madam. You speak mirth; old age is at my door, but old age is a long journey from your ladyship yet."

Livia said:

"Truly, I'm nine-and-thirty; I have lived every stroke of every hour of thirty-nine years, wench.

"And it is a general observation among knights, wives, and widows, that we account ourselves then old when young men's eyes stop looking at us.

"It is a true rule among us, and never failed yet in any but in one that I remember. Indeed, she had a friend — a lover — at nine-and-forty. By the Virgin Mary, she paid well for him; and in the end he kept a quean or two — a whore or two — with her own money, who robbed her of her plate and cut her throat."

"Plate" is silver- or gold-plated dishes and bowls.

Leantio's mother said, "She had her punishment in this world, madam, and she is a fair warning to all other women that they should live chastely at the age of fifty."

Livia replied:

"Aye, or never, wench."

In other words: Women should live chastely at fifty years of age — or never.

Readers may guess that Livia has chosen "never" for herself.

Livia continued:

"Come, now that I have thy company, I'll not part with it until after supper."

Leantio's mother said, "I must ask for your pardon, madam."

"I swear that you shall stay for supper," Livia said. "We have no strangers, woman. None will be here except my sojourners and me; my sojourners are this gentleman and the young heir: his ward. You know our company."

Leantio's mother said, "Some other time I will make bold with you, madam, and accept your invitation."

"Nay, please stay, widow," Guardiano said.

"Indeed, she shall not go," Livia said. "Do you think I'll be forsworn?"

Earlier, Livia had sworn that Leantio's mother would stay.

"It is a great while until supper time," Leantio's mother said. "So then I'll take my leave now, madam, and I will come again in the evening, since your ladyship will have it so."

Livia said:

"In the evening? Indeed, wench, I'll keep you while I have you.

"You have great business surely that requires you to sit alone at home?

"I wonder much what pleasure you take in it! If it were up to me now, I should be always at one neighbor's house or other all day long.

"Having no responsibilities, and no one to chide you, if you go or stay, who may live merrier, aye, or more at heart's ease?

"Come, we'll play chess or draughts."

"Draughts" is "checkers."

Livia continued:

"There are a hundred tricks to drive out time until supper, never fear it, wench."

"I'll just make one step home, and return straightaway, madam," Leantio's mother said.

Livia said:

"Come, I'll not trust you; you give more excuses to your kind friends than anyone I ever knew.

"What business can you have at home if you are sure you've locked the doors? And, since that is all you have to do, I know you're careful and have taken care of it.

"Is one afternoon so much time to spend here!

"Let's say that I should entreat you now to lie a night or two, or a week, with me, or leave your own house for a month together.

"It would be a kindness that long being neighbors and friends might well hope to prevail in.

"Would you deny such a request, indeed?

"Speak the truth, and freely."

"I would be then uncivil, madam," Leantio's mother said, "if I were to decline the invitation."

Livia said:

"Go, then, and set up your men."

She pointed to the chess-pieces on the chessboard.

Livia then said:

"We'll have whole nights of mirth together before we are much older, wench."

Leantio's mother said to herself, "It is as good now as to tell her then, for she will know it. I have always found her to be a most friendly lady."

"Why, widow, where's your mind?" Livia asked. "What are you thinking about?"

Leantio's mother said:

"Truly, my mind is even at home, madam.

"To tell you the truth, I left a gentlewoman even sitting all alone, which is uncomfortable, especially to young bloods — to young temperaments."

"This is another excuse," Livia said.

Leantio's mother said, "No; as I hope for health, madam, that's a truth. Please send someone to my home to see if I am telling the truth."

"What gentlewoman?" Livia said. "Bah."

Leantio's mother said, "She is my son's wife, indeed; but that relationship is not known, madam, to anyone but yourself."

"Now I beshrew and criticize you," Livia said. "Could you be so unkind to her and me as to come here and not bring her? Indeed, it is not friendly."

"I feared to be too bold," Leantio's mother said.

"Too bold!" Livia said. "Oh, what's become of the true and hearty love that used to exist among neighbors in the old times?"

"And she's a stranger, madam," Leantio's mother said.

Brancha was a foreigner: She was not a native of Florence.

Livia said:

"Then the more should be her welcome.

"When is courtesy in better practice than when it is employed in entertaining strangers? I could chide and criticize you, indeed!

"Leave her behind, poor gentlewoman! Alone, too!

"Make some amends and send for her at once; go."

Leantio's mother asked, "Will it please you to command one of your servants, madam, to go for her?"

Livia called for a servant: "Within there!"

A servant entered the room and said, "Madam."

Livia said, "Attend the gentlewoman."

Leantio's mother said to herself:

"It must be carried wondrously privately and kept secret from my son's knowledge; he'll break out in storms of rage otherwise."

She said to the servant:

"Hark you, sir. Listen."

She spoke privately to the servant, and then he exited.

Livia said quietly to Guardiano, "Now comes the heat of your part: This is the most challenging part for you to accomplish."

"True, I know it, lady," Guardiano said, "and if I should be out, may the Duke banish me from all employments, wanton or serious."

Guardiano had interpreted — as a joke — the word "part" as an actor's role. When an actor is "out," he has forgotten his lines.

Livia said out loud, "So; have you sent the servant to your home, widow?"

"Yes, madam, he's almost at my home by this time," Leantio's mother said.

Livia said:

"And indeed, let me entreat you that henceforward all such unkind faults may be swept from friendship that do but dim the luster; and think thus much it is a wrong to me, who has the ability and the wealth to bid friends welcome, when you keep them away from me.

"You cannot set greater dishonor near me, for bounty is the credit and the glory of those who have enough. I see you're sorry, and the good amends are made by it."

The servant escorted Brancha into the room.

Leantio's mother said, "Here she is, madam."

Brancha said to herself about her mother-in-law, "I wonder why she comes to send for me now?"

Livia said to her, "Gentlewoman, you're most welcome, trust me, you are, as courtesy can make one, or respect can be due to your noble appearance."

"I give you thanks, lady," Brancha said.

Livia said:

"I heard you were alone, and it had appeared an ill condition — bad manners — in me, although I didn't know you, nor ever saw you (yet humaneness and concern for others think every case their own) to have kept your company — the widow — here away from you and left you all solitary.

"I rather ventured upon boldness then, as the least fault, and wished your presence here: a thing most happily suggested by that gentleman, Guardiano, whom I request you, for his care and pity, to honor and reward with your acquaintance.

"He is a gentleman who stands for ladies' rights. That's his profession."

"A gentleman who stands" can mean "a gentleman who has an erection."

"Profession" is "what he professes."

Guardiano's profession is also the management of the rights of the Foolish Ward.

Brancha said, "It is a noble profession, and it honors my acquaintance."

Guardiano said, "All my intentions and endeavors are servants to such mistresses."

A "servant" can be a "male admirer."

A "mistress" can be a 1) a woman who is admired, and 2) a woman who has sex with someone to whom she is not married.

Brancha said, "It is your modesty, it seems, that makes your deserts speak so low, sir."

"Speak so low" can mean 1) speak quietly, 2) speak self-effacingly, and 3) speak about "low" things.

Livia said to Leantio's mother:

"Come, widow."

She then said to Brancha:

"Look, lady, here's our business: the business of the widow and me."

Livia pointed to the chessboard.

She then said:

"Aren't we well-employed, don't you think? This is an old quarrel between us that will never be at an end."

She and the widow often played chess together.

The old quarrel was also that between the white pieces and the black pieces — that is, between good and evil.

Brancha said, "No, the quarrel will never end, and I think there's men enough to part you, lady."

The chessmen would part Livia and Leantio's mother, as the two women would be on different sides of the chessboard.

Another meaning of the verb "part" is "share." Many men could part Livia's legs and share her.

According to the *Oxford English Dictionary*, as an adjective, "part" can be defined as "Divided into parts; impales."

Many men could "impale" Livia during sex.

Livia laughed:

"Ho!"

She then said:

"But they set us on, so let us come off as well as we can."

"Set us on" means 1) encourage us (to battle in chess), and/or 2) sexually excite.

"Come off" means 1) come off (the chessboard, perhaps as a winner), and/or 2) achieve orgasm.

Livia added:

"Poor souls, men care no farther.

"Please sit down, indeed, if you have the patience to look upon two weak and tedious gamesters."

Guardiano said, "Truly, madam, set these by until evening. You'll have enough of it then; the gentlewoman, being a stranger, would take more delight in seeing your rooms and pictures."

Livia said:

"By the Virgin Mary, good sir, that is well remembered. I ask you to show them to her. That will beguile and pass time well and pleasantly. Please heartily do, sir; I'll do as much for you.

"Here, take these keys."

She handed him the keys and then said:

"Show her the monument, too; that's a thing not everyone sees. You can witness that, widow."

A monument is literally a carved statue of a figure. Here, it is metaphorically the Duke.

Referring to the literal statue, Leantio's mother said, "And that's a worthy sight indeed, madam."

Brancha said to Livia, "Kind lady, I fear I came to be a trouble to you."

"Oh, nothing less, truly," Livia replied.

An obsolete meaning of "nothing less" is "not at all."

Brancha said, "And I am a trouble to this courteous gentleman, who wears a kindness in his breast so noble and bounteous to the welcome of a stranger."

Guardiano said, "If you just give acceptance to my service, you do the greatest grace and honor to me that courtesy can merit."

Guardiano's service is to the Duke, whom he will provide with an opportunity to sleep with Brancha.

"I would be to blame else, and out of fashion much," Brancha said. "Please lead the way, sir."

"After a game or two, we will join you, gentlefolks," Livia said.

Guardiano said, "We wish no better seconds in society — assistants in social activities — than your discourses, madam, and your partner's there."

Leantio's mother said, "I thank your praise, I listened to you, sir; although when you spoke, there came a paltry rook full in my way, and choked up all my game."

The rook is also called the castle, and in this society, it was sometimes called the duke.

"Game" can have a sexual meaning.

The verb "to rook" means "to cheat or swindle."

Guardiano was setting in motion the Duke's taking of Brancha's chastity.

Guardiano and Brancha exited.

"Alas, poor widow, I shall be too hard for thee," Livia said.

"You're cunning at the game, I'll be sworn, madam," Leantio's mother said.

Livia was cunning at being a procuress for the sexual games of the Duke.

Livia said, "It will be found so before I am finished with you. She who can place her man well —"

The "man" is 1) a chess piece, and 2) the Duke, who was in a place from where he would soon appear suddenly.

Leantio's mother interrupted, "— as you do, madam."

Livia said:

"As I shall, wench."

She then finished the sentence that was interrupted:

"— can never lose her game."

Leantio's mother, who was playing the white pieces, touched the black king.

Livia said:

"Nay, nay, the black king's mine."

In this society, black is the color of evil, and white is the color of good.

Leantio's mother said, "I beg your mercy, madam!"

She was apologizing for touching the wrong piece.

"And this is my queen," Livia said.

Metaphorically, Livia is the queen in the sexual game about to take place. She is a powerful woman who uses her power to achieve victories for evil.

"I see it now," Leantio's mother said.

Livia said:

"Here's a duke [rook or castle] that will strike a sure stroke — a sure blow — for the game soon."

Another kind of Duke will also soon strike and engage in sexual stroking.

Livia continued:

"Your pawn cannot come back to relieve itself."

In the game of chess, pawns can only go forward; they cannot go backwards.

In another game, Brancha will be the pawn, and she will be unable to retreat and save herself.

"I know that, madam," Leantio's mother said.

Livia said:

"You play well the while."

She then said to herself:

"How she — that is, I — belies her — that is, the widow's — skill!"

Livia then said out loud:

"I bet two ducats that I will give you check and mate to your white king, which is simplicity itself, your saintish king there."

The white king is metaphorically Leantio: the legitimate husband of Brancha.

"Simplicity" can mean "an innocent person."

Leantio's mother, "Well, before now, lady, I have seen the fall of subtlety: Jest on."

"Subtlety" is "cunning trickery."

Livia said, "Aye, but simplicity receives two for one."

Simplicity turns the other cheek and receives two blows instead of one.

Matthew 5:39-40 (King James Version) states:

39) *But I say unto you, That ye resist not evil: but whosoever shall smite thee on thy right cheek, turn to him the other also.*

40) *And if any man will sue thee at the law, and take away thy coat, let him have thy cloke [cloak] also.*

Non-believers may choose to believe that it is good to resist evil.

Leantio's mother said, "What remedy but patience!"

Guardiano and Brancha were together in a gallery.

"Trust me, sir, my eye never met with fairer ornaments," Brancha said.

"Indeed, they are livelier — that is, more lifelike — I'm persuaded, than the ornaments either Florence or Venice can produce," Guardiano said.

"Sir, my opinion supports your opinion highly," Brancha said.

"There's a better piece yet than all these," Guardiano said.

The Duke entered the scene behind Brancha, who at first did not see him.

"That is not possible, sir!" Brancha said.

"Believe it," Guardiano said. "You'll say so when you see it. Just turn your eye now and you're upon it immediately."

As Brancha saw the Duke and as Guardiano exited, she said, "Oh, sir!"

The Duke said:

"He's gone, beauty.

"Bah! Don't look after him. He's just a vapor that when the sun appears is seen no more."

"The sun" is an image often used to refer to nobility.

The Duke put his arms around Brancha.

She said, "Oh, treachery to honor!"

The Duke said:

"Please don't tremble. I feel thy breast shake like a turtledove panting under a loving hand that makes much of it and caresses it."

Although she was legally married, Brancha was only almost sixteen years old.

The Duke continued:

"Why are you so fearful? As I'm a friend to brightness and beauty, there's nothing but respect and honor near thee.

"You know me; you have seen me. Here's a heart that can witness I have seen thee."

"The more's my danger," Brancha said.

The Duke said:

"The more's thy happiness. Bah! Don't resist me, sweet."

Brancha struggled to get away from him, but he was stronger than she was.

The Duke continued:

"This strength would be excellently employed in love now, but here it is spent amiss.

"Don't strive to seek thy liberty and keep me still in prison.

"Indeed, you shall not go out, until I'm released now."

The kind of "release" he wanted was "sexual release": orgasm.

The Duke was "imprisoned" by lust.

The Duke continued:

"We'll be both freed together, or stay still imprisoned by it. So is captivity pleasant."

"Oh, my lord!" Brancha said.

The Duke said:

"I am not here in vain; have but the leisure to think about that, and thou shall soon know the outcome.

"The lifting of thy voice is just like one who exalts his enemy, who proving high, lays all the plots to confound him who raised him."

"Exalt" means "raise." Brancha, without meaning or wanting to, was raising the Duke's penis.

"Exalt" can also mean 1) praise, or 2) raise one's voice.

The Duke was talking about a person who helps someone to become a powerful man, only for that man to turn on the person who helped him.

If Brancha were to "exalt" the Duke by raising her voice and calling for help, she would make a powerful enemy.

The Duke was threatening her.

The Duke continued:

"Take warning, I tell thee.

"Thou seem to me to be a creature so composed of gentleness and delicate meekness, such as bless the faces of figures that are drawn to represent goddesses and make art proud to look upon her own work.

"I should be sorry that the least force should lay an unkind touch upon thee."

Brancha said:

"Oh, my extremity!"

She was in an extremely dangerous situation.

She then said:

"My lord, what do you seek?"

"Love," the Duke said.

"My love is bestowed already," Brancha said. "I have a husband to whom I have given it."

"That's a single comfort," the Duke said. "Take a friend in addition to him."

The kind of "friend" the Duke meant was a lover.

"That's a double mischief, or else there's no religion," Brancha said.

"Mischief" here means "evil."

The double evil is 1) envy, and 2) adultery.

Exodus 20:14 states, "*Thou shalt not commit adultery*" (King James Version).

Exodus 20:17 states, "Thou shalt not *covet thy neighbour's house,* **thou shalt not covet thy neighbour's wife***, nor his manservant, nor his maidservant, nor his ox, nor his ass, nor any thing that is thy neighbour's*" (King James Version, bold added).

The Duke said, "Do not tremble at fears of thine own making."

Definitely, Brancha had something to fear.

Does she also have a fear of her own making?

She has a fear of the Lord, aka God, and the Duke does not have that fear.

Brancha said:

"And, great lord, do not make me bold and at ease in the presence of spiritual death and deeds of ruin because they do not frighten you.

"They must frighten me.

"When they frighten me, I am in the best spiritual health.

"Should thunder speak and should no one pay it any attention, it would have lost its name and fearsome reputation, and might as well be still and silent.

"I'm not like those who take their soundest sleeps in greatest tempests. At such times when the weather is most frightening, I wake the most and call to virtue for strength."

The "voice of thunder" is metaphorically the "voice of God."

Proverbs 1:7 states, "*The fear of the LORD is the beginning of knowledge: but fools despise wisdom and instruction*" (King James Version).

Proverbs 8:13 states, "*The fear of the LORD is to hate evil: pride, and arrogancy, and the evil way, and the froward mouth, do I hate*" (King James Version).

Job 28:28 states, "*And unto man he said, Behold, the fear of the Lord, that is wisdom; and to depart from evil is understanding*" (King James Version).

The Duke said:

"To be sure, I think thou know the way to please me.

"I prefer a passionate pleading more than an easy yielding.

"But I have never pitied any pleaders. They who will not pity me deserve no pity.

"I can command. Think upon that.

"Yet if thou truly knew the infinite pleasure my affection takes in gentle, fair entreatings, when love's businesses are carried courteously between heart and heart, you'd make more haste to please me."

The Duke can command her: He can rape her. He has "never pitied any pleaders," and so he has raped women before. But the Duke was advising that Brancha have sex willingly with him because he can give her good things.

Brancha asked, "Why should you seek, sir, to take away that which you cannot give?"

The Duke can take away her chastity and good reputation, but can he give those things back to her?

He said:

"But I give better things in exchange: wealth and honor."

This kind of honor would not be virtuous; it would be respect paid to her because she is the Duke's mistress, aka whore.

The Duke continued:

"She who is fortunate in a Duke's favor, alights on a tree that bears all women's wishes. If your own mother saw you pluck fruit there, she would commend your wit and intelligence, and she would praise the time of your nativity: your birth."

The Duke did not realize it, but his words called forth the image of the snake convincing Eve to pluck the forbidden fruit in the Garden of Eden.

The Duke continued:

"Take hold of glory.

"Don't I know you've cast away your life upon necessities, means completely doubtful to keep you in merely adequate health and fashion."

Brancha had married — cast away her life, in the Duke's words — upon someone who could provide her only with necessities, and sometimes perhaps not even those.

Brancha and Leantio and his mother were poor.

The Duke continued:

"This is a thing I heard very recently, and soon pitied!

"And can you be so much your beauty's enemy, to kiss away a month or two in wedlock, and weep whole years in wants forever after?

"Come, play the wise wench, and provide for yourself forever.

"Let storms of adversity come when they wish: They will find thee sheltered.

"Should any doubt or fear arise, let nothing trouble thee: Put trust in our love for the managing of all to thy heart's peace."

"Our love"? There is no "our love." Brancha does not love the Duke, who feels lust rather than love.

The Duke concluded:

"We'll walk together and show a thankful joy for both our fortunes."

The Duke and Brancha exited.

Livia and Leantio's mother had been in the same building as the Duke and Brancha but on different floors.

Livia said, "Didn't I say my duke would fetch you over — get the better of you — widow?"

"I think you spoke in earnest when you said it, madam," Leantio's mother replied.

"And my black king makes all the haste he can, too," Livia said.

Here, the black king is figuratively the Duke.

"Well, madam, we may meet with him in time yet," Leantio's mother said.

"I have given thee blind mate twice," Livia said.

"Blind mate" is when a player makes a move that checkmates the opposing player's king but does not realize it and says only "Check" and not "Checkmate."

The Duke and Brancha were currently mating in another room, and Livia had blinded Leantio's mother to that fact by keeping her busy with chess.

"You may see, madam," Leantio's mother said. "My eyes begin to fail."

"I'll swear they do, wench," Livia said.

Livia knew that the Duke and Brancha would have sex, but Livia cannot see them, so it was a blind mate to her as well.

Guardiano entered the scene.

He said to himself:

"I can only smile as often as I think about it!

"How prettily the poor fool was beguiled. How unexpectedly! It's a witty age!"

"Witty" means "intelligent," but this age used its wit to corrupt honest wives.

Guardiano continued saying to himself:

"Never were there finer snares for women's honesties — chastities — than are devised in these days; no spider's web is made of a daintier thread than are now practiced to catch love's flesh-fly by the silver wing."

A flesh-fly deposits its eggs in rotten flesh. The Duke was depositing his semen in Brancha.

Brancha was a victim of what is probably rape. If it wasn't rape, it was as close to being rape as it could be without being rape.

Women who have been in that situation sometimes regard their flesh afterward as rotten.

Brancha had been caught by a silver wing: a gallery or wing of the house that contained many ornaments to look at.

Guardiano continued saying to himself:

"Yet, to prepare her stomach — her appetite for sex — by degrees to Cupid's feast, because I saw it was queasy, I showed her naked pictures by the way: a morsal to stay the appetite."

The queasiness was in part because of Brancha's moral scruples.

"Stay" can mean "halt," but Guardiano was using an alternative meaning, which is "strengthen."

Guardiano continued saying to himself:

"Well, advancement, I work hard to find thee.

"If thou come with a greater title set upon thy crest, I'll take that first cross patiently, and wait until some other cross comes greater than that.

"I'll endure all."

Guardiano was hoping that he would be rewarded for his work as a pander by being given a high title. If he received that reward, he would patiently bear that first cross: the pandering of Brancha. That first cross was a sin.

A cross is 1) a disappointment or vexation, and 2) the cross Christ died on for our sins.

A sin can be a cross because it can cause disappointment and vexation, if not in this life, then in the next.

Guardiano would also wait "until some other cross comes greater than that": damnation to Hell as a consequence of his sin.

Or, possibly, "the greater title" is greater than that of "pander." If Guardiano is rewarded for being a pander, he will gladly commit a greater cross (sin) later if it will advance him.

"To take the cross" means 1) to wear the cross because of a vow, and/or 2) to go on a crusade.

Guardiano was willing to take up the cross as a way of showing his support of the Duke — not support of God.

Livia said, "The game's even at the best now: You may see, widow, how all things draw to an end."

The chess game was over, and the Duke had climaxed.

Another thing drawing to an end was the life of Leantio's aged mother, as she well knew.

Leantio's mother said, "Even so I do, madam."

"Please take some of your neighbors along with you," Livia said.

Leantio's mother said, "They must be those who are almost twice your years then, if they are chosen as fit matches for my age, madam."

Livia is thirty-nine; twice her years is seventy-eight: a good age to die.

In this society, the phrase "to die" can also mean "to have an orgasm."

"Come to an end" means 1) die, and 2) come to a sexual climax.

Leantio's mother was only sixty years old, but in this society, that was old.

Livia asked, "Hasn't my duke bestirred himself?"

The duke (rook, aka castle) had bestirred itself in winning the game. The Duke had bestirred himself sexually.

"Yes, indeed, madam," Leantio's mother said. "He has done me all the mischief in this game."

The word "mischief" can mean "evil."

"He has shown himself in his kind," Livia said. "He has shown his true nature."

The duke (rook, aka castle) has shown its own nature as it moved on the chessboard. The Duke has shown his own nature as a sexual predator.

"In his kind, do you call it?" Leantio's mother said. "I may swear that."

Livia said, "Yes, indeed, you may say that and keep your oath. You will not be forsworn when you say that."

Guardiano said to himself, "Hark! Listen! There's somebody coming down. It is she."

Brancha came down from upstairs.

She said to herself:

"Now bless me and protect me from a blasting!"

A "blasting" was a withering, as of flowers. It could also be a lightning blast from an angry God. Contracting venereal disease was also a possibility.

Women often blamed and blame themselves for losing their chastity, even when forced to do so. They regarded and regard themselves as suffering a blasting, aka moral disfigurement.

Brancha continued saying to herself:

"I saw just now that which is fearful for any woman's eye to look on."

She had seen a rapist.

Brancha continued saying to herself:

"Infectious mists and mildews hang at his eyes."

This society regarded mists and fogs as unhealthy. Mildew is fungi that harm plants.

Brancha continued saying to herself:

"The weather of a doomsday dwells upon him.

"Yet since my honor is leprous, why should I preserve that fair — that beauty — that caused the leprosy?

The beauty can be the beauty of physical features, and 2) the beauty of virtue.

Brancha continued saying to herself:

"Come, poison, all at once."

She said quietly to Guardiano:

"Thou, in whose baseness the bane [poison] to virtue broods and hatches, I'm bound in soul eternally to curse thy smooth-browed, hypocritical treachery — treachery that wore the fair veil of a friendly welcome, and I was a stranger."

Leviticus 19:34 states, *"But the stranger that dwelleth with you shall be unto you as one born among you, and thou shalt love him as thyself; for ye were strangers in the land of Egypt: I am the LORD your God"* (King James Version).

Hebrews 13:2 states, *"Be not forgetful to entertain strangers: for thereby some have entertained angels unawares"* (King James Version).

"Veil" calls to mind "vail." Gentlemen would vail — take off — their hats to greet someone.

"Smooth-browed" means "appearing to be innocent."

Brancha continued saying quietly to Guardiano:

"Think upon it. It is worth thinking about.

"Murders piled upon a guilty spirit at his last breath will not lie heavier than this betraying act upon thy conscience.

"Beware of offering the first fruits to sin."

The first fruits are to be offered to God, not to sin.

Proverbs 3:9 states, *Honor the LORD with thy substance, and with thy firstfruits of all thy increase:* (King James Version).

The first fruits are part of the first harvest.

If the Duke were to get Brancha pregnant, her first fruit would be the Duke's baby.

Brancha continued saying quietly to Guardiano:

"His weight is deadly who commits fornication with strumpets."

The weight is literally the weight of the man on top of the woman in the missionary position.

The weight can also be figuratively the spiritual weighing down of his guilty soul to Hell.

Brancha continued saying quietly to Guardiano:

"After they — the strumpets — have been abased and made for use as whores, if those who use whores offend to the death and commit deadly sin, as wise men know that those men do, how much guiltier then are they who first make the strumpets whores?

"I give thee that to feed on and think about."

Brancha did not use the respectful "you" as she spoke to Guardiano.

Guardiano was the man who had set up the situation that resulted in the loss of Brancha's honor and chastity. If Brancha was guilty and had offended to the death of the soul and deserved punishment in Hell, Guardiano deserved such punishment much more than Brancha did.

Even though Brancha had been raped, she regarded herself as a strumpet and a whore.

Brancha continued saying quietly to Guardiano:

"I'm made bold now, for which I thank thy treachery.

"Sin and I are acquainted; no couple are greater and better acquainted. And I'm like that great one, who making politic — crafty — use of a base villain, likes the treason well, but hates the traitor; so I hate thee, slave!"

If Brancha is like the great one who "likes the treason well," does that mean she enjoyed the sex?

Or is she making an imperfect comparison? She certainly did not make politic use of a base villain.

Or did she? Or will she, perhaps?

Perhaps Brancha saw Livia's many possessions and was reminded of the good things that wealth and power can provide. Becoming the Duke's mistress would allow her to have access to those things. And if she felt self-contempt because of what had happened to her, she may have decided to at least enjoy those things.

The Duke is a rich and powerful man. She could become his mistress in hopes of becoming his wife. The Duke is a widower who has not yet remarried. Brancha may hate Guardiano, yet she may learn to enjoy being the Duke's mistress and sharing his wealth.

Guardiano replied quietly, "Well, as long as the Duke loves me, I fare not much amiss then. Two great feasts seldom come together in one day. We must not look for them."

Guardiano will have one great feast. It will come from the Duke and not from Brancha.

Brancha then asked out loud, "What, at it still, mother?"

"You see we sit by the chessboard," Leantio's mother replied. "Are you so soon returned?"

Livia said to herself, "She is so lively, and so cheerful; that is a good sign."

"You have not seen everything since you left, surely?" Leantio's mother asked Brancha.

Brancha said:

"That have I, mother. I saw the monument and all."

The monument was the Duke.

Brancha continued:

"I'm so beholden to this 'kind, honest, courteous' gentleman."

She was referring — with irony — to Guardiano.

Brancha continued:

"You'd little think it, mother; he showed me everything. He had me from place to place so fashionably."

"Had me" means "brought me." In addition, the Duke "had" her sexually.

Brancha continued speaking with irony:

"The 'kindness' of some people — how it exceeds!

"Indeed, I have seen that which I scarcely thought to see in the morning when I rose."

Leantio's mother replied:

"Nay, so I told you before you saw it that it would prove worth your sight."

She then said to Guardiano:

"I give you great thanks for my daughter, sir, and all your kindness towards her."

Guardiano said out loud:

"Oh! Good widow, much good may it do her —"

He then said quietly to himself:

"— forty weeks from now, indeed."

Forty weeks is roughly nine months: the length of a pregnancy.

A servant entered the scene.

Livia asked, "What is the news now, sir?"

The servant said, "May it please you, madam, to walk in? Supper's upon the table."

Livia said to the servant:

"Yes, we come."

She then asked Brancha:

"Will it please you to go in, gentlewoman?"

Brancha replied out loud:

"Thanks, virtuous lady."

She then said quietly to Livia:

"You're a damned bawd."

"Damned" meant "damned to Hell." This society took Christianity seriously.

Brancha then said out loud:

"I'll follow you, indeed.

"Please take my mother in."

She then said quietly to Livia:

"An old ass goes with you, Livia."

Brancha was angry at her mother-in-law, who had not known to protect her.

Brancha then said out loud:

"This 'gentleman' and I vow not to part."

"This gentleman" is Guardiano.

Livia said, "Then get you both before."

In other words: You two go inside first.

Brancha said to herself, "There lies his art."

As a pandar, Guardiano shows up first, and then the Duke shows up.

Brancha, Guardiano, and the servant exited.

Livia said, "Widow, I'll follow you."

Leantio's mother exited.

Alone, Livia said to herself:

"Is it so! 'Damned bawd!'"

"Are you, Brancha, so bitter?"

"It is only because of lack of use."

"Lack of use" means "you have not yet become accustomed to being used as a whore."

Livia continued saying to herself:

"Her tender modesty is sea-sick a little because she is not accustomed to the breaking billow of Woman's wavering faith, blown with temptations.

"It is only a qualm of honor; it will go away.

"It is a little bitter for the time, but it does not last.

"Sin tastes at the first draught like wormwood water.

"But drunk again, it is nectar ever after."

"Wormwood water" is made from wormwood, a bitter herb.

According to Livia, the first time a woman is forced to commit adultery, it leaves a bitter taste, but the woman soon grows to like it.

Nectar is the drink of the Greek and Roman gods.

Livia exited.

CHAPTER 3

— 3.1 —

Alone, Leantio's mother said to herself:

"I wish my son would either stay at home or I were in my grave!

"Brancha was only one day out of the house, but ever since she's grown so cutted — that is, cross and curt — there's no speaking to her.

"Whether the sight of great cheer — good food and entertainment — at my Lady Livia's house and such mean, poor fare at home, work discontent in her, I don't know, but I'm sure she's strangely altered.

"I'll never keep a daughter-in-law in the house with me again, even if I had a hundred.

"When did I ever read of any who agreed together and lived in harmony for a long time? Instead, she and her mother-in-law fell out in the first quarter of a year; nay, sometimes a grudging — a small amount — of a scolding started the first week, by Our Lady — the Virgin Mary! So catches hold the new disease, I think, in my house."

A grudging of a disease is its first sign. The new disease is Brancha's sudden disagreeable manner.

Leantio's mother continued saying to herself:

"I'm weary of my part; there's nothing that pleases her. I don't know how to please her here lately.

"And here she comes."

Brancha entered the scene and complained to her mother-in-law:

"This is the strangest house for all defects as ever a gentlewoman had to put up with, to pass away her love in.

"Why isn't there a cushion-covering of drawn work, or some fair cut-work pinned up in my bed-chamber?"

These were wall hangings and furniture that Leantio and his mother could not afford.

"Drawn" work was a kind of ornament in a cushion-covering; the ornamental design was created by drawing out some threads to form a pattern.

"Cut-work" was lace with a pattern cut into it.

Brancha continued complaining to her mother-in-law:

"Why isn't there a silver and gilt casting bottle hung by it?"

A casting bottle was used to sprinkle perfume.

Brancha continued complaining to her mother-in-law:

"Indeed, I should have them since I am content to be so kind to you as to spare you the trouble of providing me with a silver basin and ewer, which one of my fashion looks for as due to her. She's never offered less where she sleeps."

A ewer is a water pitcher.

Leantio's mother said to herself, "She talks about things now that are more expensive than my whole estate's worth."

Brancha continued complaining to her mother-in-law:

"Isn't there a green silk quilt in the house, mother, to cast upon my bed?"

Leantio's mother said, "No, indeed, there is not. Nor is there an orange-tawny quilt."

The color "orange-tawny" was associated with courtiers.

Brancha said sarcastically, "Here's a house for a young gentlewoman to be begotten with child in!"

Leantio's mother said:

"Yes, simple though you consider it, there has been three begotten in a year in it, since you anger me into saying it, and all were as sweet-faced children, and as lovely as you'll be mother of — I will not spare you my comment!"

Three children begotten in a year! Leantio's mother must be exaggerating out of anger at Brancha. Or she may have had boarders.

Leantio's mother continued:

"What! Can't children be begotten, do you think, without gilt casting bottles? Yes, they can, and as sweet ones as those begotten with casting bottles."

Leantio's mother continued:

"The miller's daughter brings forth boys as white as those of a woman who bathes herself with milk and bean-flour."

A miller mills flour, and boys covered with flour would be white.

This society valued light skin.

Bean-flour was milled from the bean plant.

To bathe in milk and bean-flour would be a luxury. Many impoverished people would call it a waste of good food.

Leantio's mother continued:

"It is an old saying: One may keep good cheer in a mean, lowly house. So may true love affect people in a cottage as much as true love affects princes."

A proverb stated, "Content lodges oftener in cottages than in palaces."

Brancha complained:

"Indeed, you speak wondrously well about your old house here.

"It will shortly fall down at your feet to thank you, or stoop, when you go to bed, like a good child, to ask for your blessing."

"Stoop" means 1) bow, or kneel, or 2) fall down.

Brancha continued complaining:

"Must I live in want because my fortune matched me with your son?

"Wives do not give away themselves to husbands with the intention to be quite cast away; they look to be the better treated, and cherished rather, more highly respected, and richer maintained.

"They're well rewarded else for the free gift of their whole life to a husband.

"I ask for less now than what I had at home when I was a maiden, and at my father's house, where I was kept short of that which a wife knows she must have, and will have. She will have that, mother, if she is not a born fool.

"And gossip said that I could wrangle for what I wanted when I was two hours old, and by that copy, this land still I hold.

"You hear me, mother."

Brancha would not give up wrangling for what she wanted. She was like a property owner. A copyhold is right of ownership by custom of the manor. Such ownership is recorded on court-rolls. Since she was two hours old, Brancha has been wrangling for what she wanted.

Brancha exited.

Alone, Leantio's mother said to herself:

"Aye, I hear you too plainly, I think.

"And I wish that I were somewhat deafer when you spoke.

"It would be never a bit the worse for my quietness."

Her quietness would be 1) her not hearing Brancha speaking and not hearing herself speaking, and/or 2) her ease and comfort.

Not hearing Brancha's words just now would have saved her some unhappiness.

Leantio's mother continued saying to herself:

"It is the most sudden, strangest alteration, and the most subtle and hard to explain that ever wit at threescore years was puzzled to find out.

"I know no cause for it, but she's no more like the gentlewoman who first came here than I am like a girl who has never yet lay with a man — and she's a very young thing wherever she is.

"When Brancha first alighted here, I told her then how mean and lowly she would find all things; she was pleased, indeed — no one was better pleased than she.

"I laid open all defects to her. She was contented still, but the devil's in her. Nothing contents her now.

"Tonight my son promised to be at home. I wish that he had already come, for I'm weary of my charge, and I'm weary of my life, too.

"She'd be served all in silver if she had her will, by night and day. She hates the name of pewterer, more than sick men who hate noise, or diseased bones that quake at the fall of the hammer, seeming to have a fellow-feeling with it at every blow."

Pewter was an inexpensive metal used for making utensils. It was much less expensive than gold and silver, and the pewterer hammered it.

Leantio's mother continued saying to herself:

"What course of action shall I decide on? She frets me so."

She exited.

Leantio entered the room his mother had vacated.

Alone, he said to himself:

"How near am I now to a happiness that the earth does not exceed!

"There is not another like it. The treasures of the deep are not as precious as are the concealed comforts and hidden blessings of a man locked up in a woman's love.

"I scent the air of blessings when I come just near the house. What a delicious breath marriage sends forth! The violet-bed's not sweeter.

"Honest wedlock is like a banqueting-house built in a garden. On the banqueting-house, the spring's chaste flowers take delight to cast their modest odors."

Many gardens had buildings in the garden in which a meal could be eaten. In Elizabethan and Jacobean plays, these buildings were often used for assignations.

Leantio continued saying to himself:

"Whereas base lust, with all her powders, cosmetics, and best finery, is only a fair house built beside a ditch side — beside an open sewer.

"When I behold a glorious dangerous strumpet, sparkling in beauty and in destruction, too, both at a twinkling, I do liken immediately her beautified body to a goodly temple that is built on vaults where carcasses lie rotting."

Matthew 23:27 states, "*Woe unto you, scribes and Pharisees, hypocrites! for ye are like unto whited sepulchres, which indeed appear beautiful outward, but are within full of dead men's bones, and of all uncleanness*" (King James Version).

Leantio continued saying to himself:

"And so, by little and little, I shrink back again, and quench desire with a cool meditation."

Leantio shrinks back away from the whore, and his penis also shrinks.

Leantio continued saying to himself:

"And I'm as well again as I was before I saw the whore, I think.

"Now for a welcome that is able to draw men's envies upon a man: A kiss now that will hang upon my lip, as sweet as morning dew upon a rose, and fully as long."

Dew quickly evaporates.

Leantio continued saying to himself:

"After a five days' fast, she'll be so greedy now, and cling about me. I worry how I shall be rid of her."

Brancha and Leantio's mother entered the scene.

Leantio continued saying to himself:

"And here it begins."

Brancha did not kiss him, but she did say, "Oh, sir, you're welcome home."

"Oh, has he come?" Leantio's mother said. "I am glad of it."

Leantio said to himself about Brancha's cordial but distant greeting:

"Is that all? Why this lack of affection? It is as dreadful now as sudden death to some rich man, who flatters — that is, excuses — all his sins with the promise of repentance when he's old —"

Saint Augustine once prayed, "O Lord, give me chastity, but do not give it yet."

Leantio continued saying to himself:

"— and dies in the midpoint of life before he comes to repentance."

Luke 12:15-21 (King James Version) states:

15) *And he said unto them, Take heed, and beware of covetousness: for a man's life consisteth not in the abundance of the things which he possesseth.*

16) *And he spake a parable unto them, saying, The ground of a certain rich man brought forth plentifully:*

17) *And he thought within himself, saying, What shall I do, because I have no room where to bestow my fruits?*

18) *And he said, This will I do: I will pull down my barns, and build greater; and there will I bestow all my fruits and my goods.*

19) *And I will say to my soul, Soul, thou hast much goods laid up for many years; take thine ease, eat, drink, and be merry.*

20) *But God said unto him, Thou fool, this night thy soul shall be required of thee: then whose shall those things be, which thou hast provided?*

21) *So is he that layeth up treasure for himself, and is not rich toward God.*

Leantio said out loud:

"Surely, you're not well, Brancha! How are you, please?"

"I have been better than I am at this time," Brancha said.

"Alas, I thought so," Leantio said.

"Nay, I have been worse, too," Brancha said, "than now you see me, sir."

Brancha was better before she had sex with the Duke of Florence, and she was worse when she had sex with the Duke of Florence.

Leantio said:

"I'm glad thou are getting better yet. I feel my heart mend, too.

"How came thy illness to thee? Has anything displeased thee in my absence?"

Brancha said, "No, certainly I have had the best content that Florence can afford."

Florence is the city. It is also the Duke of Florence.

Leantio said:

"Thou make the best of it.

"Speak, mother, what's the cause? You must necessarily know."

Leantio's mother said:

"Truly I know no cause, son; let her speak for herself."

She then said to herself:

"Unless the cause is the same thing that gave Lucifer a tumbling cast, and that's pride."

A "cast" is a throw: Lucifer was thrown out of Heaven.

A "tumble" can be sex.

Brancha complained:

"I think this house stands nothing to my mind: It is poorly located, I think.

"I'd have some pleasant lodging in the high street, sir; or if it were near the court, sir, that would be much better.

"It is a sweet recreation for a gentlewoman to stand in a bay-window and see gallants."

Whores displayed themselves in bay-windows.

Leantio said, "Now I have another temper — a different mood — a complete stranger to that of yours, it seems. I should delight to see none but yourself."

Brancha said:

"I do not praise that.

"To be too fond and doting is as unseemly as to be too churlish and ungracious. I would not have a husband of that proneness to kiss me before company, for all the world."

"Proneness" means "eagerness," and it refers to sex in the prone position.

Brancha continued:

"Besides, it is tedious to see one thing always, sir, even if it is the best thing that ever heart affected."

A "thing" can be a penis.

"Affected" means "loved."

Brancha continued:

"Nay, were it yourself, whose love you know had the power to bring me away from my friends, I would not stand thus and gaze upon you always; truly, I could not, sir.

"It would be as good to be blind, and have no use of sight, as to look on one thing continually.

"What's the eye's treasure but change of objects?

"You are learned, sir, and you know I do not speak ill; it is fully as virtuous for a woman's eye to look on several men, as for her heart, sir, to be fixed on one."

Leantio requested, "Now thou come home to me — give me a kiss for that word."

The word is "one" in "her heart ... fixed on one" man.

Brancha said:

"There is no occasion for a kiss, sir; let it pass. It is only a trifle, we'll not so much as think about it.

"Let's change the subject and talk of other business and forget it.

"What is the news now about the pirates? Are any pirates stirring?

"Please discourse about pirates a little."

She wanted to change the subject of discussion.

Leantio's mother said to herself, "I am glad he's here now to see her tricks himself; I would have been told that I lied monstrously if I had told them to him before he witnessed them."

Leantio said to Brancha, "Speak, what's the mood, sweet, for why you make your lip so strange? What mood is this? This was not customary with you."

Brancha said:

"Is there no kindness between man and wife, unless they make a pigeon-house — a dove-cote — of friendship, and be always billing and kissing?

"It is the idlest fondness that ever was invented; and it is a pity that it has grown to be a fashion for poor gentlewomen.

"There's many a disease kissed in a year by it, and a French curtsey made to it."

The "French disease" is syphilis.

Brancha continued:

"Alas, sir, think of the world, and how we shall live. Grow serious. We have been married a whole fortnight now."

A fortnight is two weeks.

"What!" Leantio said. "A whole fortnight! Why, is that so long?"

Brancha said, "It is time to leave off dalliance; it is a doctrine of your own teaching, if you remember, and I was bound to obey it."

The honeymoon period was over.

Leantio's mother said to herself:

"Here's one who fits him: She hurts him and gives him fits.

"This was well caught, in faith, son, like a fellow who rids another country of a plague and brings it home with him to his own house."

Leantio had brought Brancha from Venice to his own house in Florence.

Knocking sounded.

Leantio's mother asked out loud:

"Who is knocking?"

Leantio said:

"Who's there now?

"Withdraw, Brancha. Thou are a gem no stranger's eye must see; however, thou were pleased just now to look dully at me."

Brancha exited.

A messenger entered the scene.

Leantio said:

"You're welcome, sir; to whom is your business, please?"

"To one I don't see here now," the messenger said.

"Who should that be, sir?" Leantio said.

"A young gentlewoman whom I was sent to," the messenger said.

"A young gentlewoman?" Leantio asked.

The only young gentlewoman in the house was Brancha.

"Aye, sir, about sixteen," the messenger said. "Why do you look so wildly, sir?"

"At your strange error," Leantio said. "You've come to the wrong house, sir. There's none such here, I assure you."

"I assure you, too, that the man who sent me cannot be mistaken," the messenger said.

In other words: The man who sent me cannot make a mistake, and he cannot be mistaken for someone else.

"Why, who is it who sent you, sir?" Leantio asked.

"The Duke," the messenger said.

"The Duke?" Leantio asked.

"Yes, he entreats her company at a banquet at Lady Livia's house," the messenger said.

Leantio said:

"Truly, I shall tell you, sir, that it is the most erroneous business that your honest pains were ever abused with.

"Please forgive me if I smile a little. I cannot choose not to smile, indeed, sir, at an error as comical as this.

"I mean no harm, though.

"His grace has been most wondrously ill informed. Please return to him and tell him this, sir.

"What is her name supposed to be?"

The messenger said, "That I shall tell you immediately, too — Brancha Capella."

"What, sir! Brancha?" Leantio said. "What do you call the other name?"

"Capella," the messenger said. "Sir, it seems you know no such person then."

"Who should this person be?" Leantio said. "I never heard of the name."

"Then it is surely a mistake," the messenger said.

"What if you enquired in the next street, sir?" Leantio said. "I saw gallants there in the new houses that were built recently. Ten to one, there you will find her."

"Nay, it doesn't matter," the messenger said. "I will return and say there was a mistake and seek her no further."

Leantio said:

"Use your own will and pleasure, sir. Do what you want.

"You're welcome."

The messenger exited.

Leantio then said to himself:

"What shall I think of to do first!"

He called:

"Come forth, Brancha."

Brancha entered the room.

Leantio said to her:

"Thou are betrayed, I fear."

"Betrayed!" Brancha said. "How, sir?

"The Duke knows thee," Leantio said.

Brancha said:

"Knows me!"

She was thinking of "know" in the Biblical sense.

Brancha then asked:

"How do you know that, sir?"

"He has gotten thy name," Leantio said.

Brancha said to herself, "Aye, and my good name, too. That's the worse of the two."

Losing her good reputation was worse than the Duke knowing her name.

"How did this come about?" Leantio asked.

"How should the Duke know me?" Brancha said. "Can you guess, mother?"

Leantio's mother said, "Not I with all my wits; to be sure, we stayed concealed in the house."

Of course, she was lying to her son.

Leantio said:

"Kept concealed at home! Not all the locks in Italy can keep you women at home; you have been gadding about, and you have ventured out at twilight, to the court-green yonder, and you have met the gallant bowlers coming home."

Lawn-bowling was a game that members of the upper class played on a bowling-green. This green was probably near the court.

Leantio continued:

"You were without your masks, too, both of you! I'll be hanged if you were wearing them!"

In this society, women wore masks and/or veils outside.

Leantio continued:

"Thou have been seen, Brancha, by some stranger. Don't try to excuse and deny it."

Brancha said:

"I'll not make excuses, sir.

"Do you think you've married me to mew — lock — me up and imprison me not to be seen?"

Hawks were mewed up — kept in a cage. In this society, as shown in William Shakespeare's *The Taming of the Shrew*, training a wife was compared to taming a hawk.

Brancha continued:

"What would you make of me?"

"A good wife, nothing else," Leantio said.

"Why, so are some who are seen every day," Brancha said. "If they aren't good wives, let the devil take them to Hell for committing adultery."

Leantio said:

"No more, then!

"I believe all virtuous in thee, without any argument or proof. It was just thy hard chance — thy bad luck — to be seen somewhere. There lies all the mischief — all the evil.

"But I have devised a remedy."

Leantio's mother said, "Now I can tell you, son, the time and place."

"When? Where?" Leantio asked.

Leantio's mother said:

"What wits have I! I have been dense, but I remember now.

"When you last took your leave, if you remember, you left us both at a window."

"Right, I know that," Leantio said.

Leantio's mother said, "And not the third part of an hour after — not twenty minutes later — the Duke passed by, in great ceremony, as he went to St. Mark's Temple, and to my knowledge he looked up twice to the window."

It was Brancha who had thought the Duke looked up to the window.

Leantio said, "Oh, there quickened — began — the mischief of this hour!"

The word "quickened" can refer to pregnancy.

In this society, "mischief" has a strong meaning: evil.

Brancha said to herself, "If you call it mischief, it is a thing I fear I am conceived with."

The word "conceived" can refer to pregnancy.

Leantio said, "He looked up twice, and you could take no warning from that?"

Leantio's mother said:

"Why, once may do as much harm, son, as a thousand.

"Don't you know that one spark has set on fire a house, as well as a whole furnace has done so?"

Leantio said:

"My heart flames for it. Yet let's be wise and keep all smothered closely."

"Smothered closely" means 1) fully concealed, and 2) smother the fire so that it goes out.

Leantio continued:

"I have thought of a means: Is the door fastened?"

Leantio's mother said, "I locked it myself after the messenger left."

Leantio said:

"You know, mother, that at the end of the dark parlor there's a place so artfully contrived for a conveyance — a secret passage — that no search could ever find it; when my father kept himself inside to escape being arrested because of manslaughter, it was his sanctuary.

"There I will lock up my life's best treasure: Brancha."

Brancha said:

"Would you keep me closer and more concealed yet?

"Have you the conscience? You're best even to choke me, sir."

"Choke" means 1) smother, or 2) throttle.

Brancha continued:

"You make me fearful of your health and wits because you cleave to such wild courses and extravagant tricks.

"What's the matter?"

Leantio said:

"Why, are you so insensible of your danger to ask that now?

"The Duke himself has sent for you to go to Lady Livia's, to a banquet, indeed."

A banquet was a light meal with sweets.

Brancha said:

"Now I beshrew and curse you heartily! Has he done so!

"And you are the man who would never yet grant to tell me about it until now.

"You show your loyalty and honesty at once; and so farewell, sir."

"Brancha, to where are you going now?" Leantio asked.

"Why, to the Duke, sir," Brancha said. "You say he sent for me."

"But thou do not mean to go, I hope," Leantio said.

Brancha said:

"No? I shall prove to be unmannerly, rude, uncivil, and mad, if I imitate you.

"Come, mother, come, follow his humor — his mood — no longer.

"We shall be all executed for treason shortly."

Leantio's mother said:

"Not I, indeed! I'll first obey the Duke and taste a good banquet. I'm of the same mind as thee.

"I'll just step upstairs and fetch two handkerchiefs to pocket some sweetmeats and overtake thee."

The handkerchiefs were used to carry small items. Leantio's mother was going to take some sweets from Lydia's house and carry them back home.

Leantio's mother went upstairs.

Brancha said to herself, "Why, here's an old wench who would trot — turn — into a bawd now for some dry sucket, or a colt in marchpane."

A sucket is crystallized fruit. A colt in marchpane is the figure of a colt created out of marzipan. Marzipan is made from ground almonds, egg whites, and sugar.

Brancha exited.

Alone, Leantio said to himself:

"Oh, thou, wedlock, are the ripe time of man's misery when all his thoughts, like over-laden trees, crack with the fruits they bear, in worries, in jealousies!

"Oh, worry is a fruit that ripens hastily, after it is joined to marriage. It begins as soon as the sun shines upon the bride a little to show color and to begin to ripen."

A bride outdoors without a mask or a veil would soon show color: sunburn or suntan.

Leantio continued saying to himself:

"Blessed powers!

"Whence comes this alteration? The distractions, the fears, and the doubts it brings are numberless, and yet I don't know the cause.

"What a peace has he who never marries!

"If he knew the benefit he enjoyed, or if he had the fortune to come and speak with me, he would know then the infinite wealth he had, and discern rightly the greatness of his treasure by my loss.

"What a quietness above mine has the man who wears his youth out in a strumpet's arms, and never spends more care upon a woman than at the time of lust, but walks away."

"Spends" also means "expends" — that is, ejaculates.

Leantio continued saying to himself:

"And if that man finds her dead at his return, his pity is soon done; he breaks a sigh into many parts and gives her only a piece of it!

"But all the fears, shames, jealousies, costs and troubles, and continually renewed cares and worries of a marriage bed live in the issue — the children — when the wife is dead."

The messenger returned and said to Leantio, "A good perfection — a successful conclusion — to your thoughts."

"What is the news, sir?" Leantio asked.

The messenger said:

"Although you were pleased recently to pin an error on me, you must not shift another in your stead, too. You must not try to play another trick to save yourself by sending me after someone else.

"The Duke has sent me for you."

Leantio said:

"What! For me, sir?"

He said to himself:

"I see then it is my theft; we're both betrayed, Brancha and I.

"Well, I'm not the first who has stolen away — that is, eloped with — a maiden. My countrymen have done it."

Leantio was assuming that the Duke wanted to see him because he had eloped with Brancha.

He said to the messenger:

"I'll go along with you, sir."

They exited.

— 3.3 —

A banquet had been prepared and set out in Livia's house.

Guardiano and the Foolish Ward entered the banquet room. Guardiano had invited Isabella to the banquet so the Foolish Ward could see her.

Guardiano said:

"Take special note of such a gentlewoman. She's here on purpose. I have invited her, her father, and her uncle to this banquet. Observe her behavior well, it does concern you; and observe closely what her good parts are. As far as time and place can modestly require a knowledge of them, her good parts shall be laid open to your understanding."

Some of Isabella's good parts are between her legs.

Guardiano continued:

"You know I'm both your guardian and your uncle. My care of you is double, ward and nephew, and I'll express and show it here."

The Foolish Ward said:

"Indeed, I should know her now by her mark — her distinctive appearance — among a thousand women.

"She is a little, pretty, dainty, and tidy thing, you say?"

"Right," Guardiano said.

"And she has a lusty — large — sprouting sprig in her hair?" the Foolish Ward asked.

He was asking whether she was wearing flowers and leaves in her hair.

Guardiano said:

"Thou go the right way still; take note of one distinguishing mark more.

"Thou shall never find her hand out of her uncle's hand, or else his out of hers, if she is near him. The love of kindred never yet stuck closer than theirs to one another; he who weds her marries her uncle's heart, too."

Cornets sounded.

"Do you say so, sir?" the Foolish Ward said. "Then I'll be asked in the church to both of them."

He would have the banns of marriage called for both Isabella and Hippolito, her uncle.

"Fall back," Guardiano said. "Here comes the Duke. Make room for him."

87

"He brings a gentlewoman, for whom I would rather fall forward," the Foolish Ward said.

He would prefer to "fall forward" into the missionary position for sex.

The Duke entered the scene, leading in Brancha, and followed by Fabritio, Hippolito, Livia, Leantio's mother, Isabella, and some attendants.

The Duke said:

"Come, Brancha, who was on purpose sent into the world to show perfection once in a woman.

"I'll believe henceforward about women that every one of them has a soul, too, against all the uncourteous opinions that man's uncivil rudeness ever held of them."

Some writers of the time believed that women did not have souls because Genesis does not record God breathing a soul into Eve. And some people used this as an insult against women.

The Duke continued:

"Glory of Florence, alight into my arms!"

Leantio, Brancha's husband, entered the scene and walked toward Branch and the Duke.

Seeing him, Brancha said:

"Yonder comes a man with a grudge who will chide and rebuke you, sir.

"The storm is now in his heart, and the storm would get nearer, and fall here if it dared to. It pours down yonder."

The Duke was powerful, and Leantio was afraid of him.

"If that is he, the weather shall soon clear," the Duke said. "Listen, and I'll tell thee how."

He whispered to Brancha.

Leantio said to himself:

"They are kissing, too!"

Possibly, Leantio was misinterpreting the Duke's whispering to Brancha. Also possibly, the Duke and Brancha were kissing.

Leantio continued saying to himself:

"I see that it is plain lust now: adultery emboldened.

"What will it prove to be soon, when it is stuffed full of wine and sweetmeats, being so impudent and immodest while fasting?"

The Duke said to Leantio:

"We have heard of your good qualities, sir, which we honor with our embrace and love."

He asked a gentleman:

"Is the captainship of Rouans citadel, since the late deceased, occupied by any yet?"

The Duke was going to bribe Leantio with the captainship.

"Rouans" sounds somewhat like "ruins." The Duke may be making Leantio the captain of a ruined citadel.

"The position is occupied by none, my lord," the gentleman replied.

The Duke said to Leantio, who was kneeling:

"Take it, the place is yours then, and as faithfulness and desert grows, our favor shall grow with it.

"Rise, now, the captain of our fort at Rouans."

Leantio replied, "May the service of my whole life give your grace thanks."

"Come sit, Brancha," the Duke said.

All sat down to enjoy the banquet.

Leantio, who was aware that he had just been bribed not to quarrel about being made a cuckold, said to himself:

"This is some good yet, and more than ever I looked for: a tasty morsel to appease a cuckold's stomach."

A cuckold is a man with an unfaithful wife.

Leantio continued saying to himself:

"All preferment that springs from sin and lust shoots up quickly, as gardeners' crops do in the rottenest grounds. So is all profit that is raised from base prostitution just like a salad growing upon a dunghill.

"I'm like a thing that never was yet heard of: half merry and half mad. I'm much like a fellow who eats his food with a good appetite and wears a plague-sore that would frighten a country."

Leantio was saying that he was like a man with a good appetite who was actually very ill.

Leantio continued saying to himself:

"Or rather I'm like the stupid hardened ass that feeds on thistles until he bleeds again, and such is the condition of my misery."

A proverb stated, "An ass may carry gold, but it still eats thistles."

Livia asked Leantio's mother, "Is that your son, widow?"

"Yes," Leantio's mother said. "Didn't your ladyship ever know that until now?"

Livia answered:

"No, trust me, I didn't."

She then said to herself:

"Nor ever truly felt the power of love, and pity to a man, until now I know him.

"I have enough to buy myself my desires, and yet have some left to spare; that's one good comfort."

Livia then said to Leantio:

"Please let me speak with you, sir, before you go."

Leantio replied:

"With me, lady? You shall, I am at your service."

Leantio then said to himself:

"What will she say now, I wonder? More gifts yet?"

Looking at Isabella, the Foolish Ward said to himself:

"I see her now, I'm sure. The ape's so little, I shall scarcely feel her."

Possibly, the Foolish Ward was complaining that Isabella was so small that she would have a short vagina.

Definitely, the Foolish Ward was criticizing Isabella, who was a small woman.

The Foolish Ward continued:

"I have seen dolls almost as tall as she sold in the fair for tenpence.

"See how she simpers, as if marmalade would not melt in her mouth; she might have the kindness, indeed, to send me a gilded bull from her own platter — a ram, a goat, or something to be nibbling."

Sweetmeats were often molded into the shapes of animals.

Bulls, rams, and goats all had the reputation of being lecherous. They also all have horns.

Leantio was now figuratively wearing the invisible horns that people in this society said that cuckolds wore.

The Foolish Ward continued:

"These women, when they come to sweet things once, they forget all their friends; they grow so greedy.

"Often, they forget their husbands."

The Duke said, "Here's a health — a toast — now, gallants, to the best beauty on this day in Florence."

"Whoever she is, she shall not go unpledged — untoasted — sir," Brancha modestly said.

"Nay, you're excused for this," the Duke said.

"Who?" Brancha said. "I, my lord?"

"Yes, by the law of Bacchus," the Duke said. "Plead your benefit and claim exemption from the law. You are not bound to pledge your own health, lady."

"That's a good way, my lord, to keep me dry," Brancha said.

By "dry," she meant "without a drink."

The Duke said:

"Nay, then I will not offend Venus so much."

The Duke was taking the word "dry" as describing Brancha's vagina.

Venus is associated with the qualities warm and wet.

The Duke continued:

"Let Bacchus seek his amends — his due privileges —in another court.

"Here's to thyself, Brancha."

"Nothing comes more welcome to that name than your grace," Brancha said.

The word "come" can mean "cum."

Watching the Duke and Brancha, Leantio said to himself:

"So, so.

"Here stands the poor thief — me — now who stole the treasure that is Brancha, and he's not thought about. I and people like me are near kin now to a twin misery born into the world.

"First the hard conscienced worldling, he hoards wealth up.

"Then comes the next generation, and the miser's heir feasts all upon it.

"One's damned for getting it, the other for spending it."

Leantio was damned for the sin of eloping with Brancha, and the Duke was damned for the sin of committing adultery with her.

Leantio continued saying to himself:

"Oh! Equal and impartial justice, thou have met my sin with a full weight.

"I'm rightly now oppressed.

"All her family's and friends' heavy hearts lie in my breast."

Leantio had sinned by eloping with Brancha, thereby causing pain to her family and friends. Now he was punished by feeling as much pain as they felt.

Leantio had stolen Brancha from her family; now the Duke was stealing Brancha from him.

The Duke said, "I think there is no spirit among us gallants, except what divinely sparkles from the eyes of bright Brancha; we would all be sitting in darkness, if not for that splendor. Who was it told us lately about a match-making rite: a formal offer of marriage?"

In Florence at the time, high-ranking grooms and brides would be presented to the Duke.

"It was I, my lord," Guardiano said.

"It was you indeed," the Duke said. "Where is she?"

"This is the gentlewoman," Guardiano said.

Fabritio and Isabella went over to the Duke.

Fabritio said, "My lord, this is my daughter."

"Why, here's some stirring yet," the Duke said.

"Stirring" can mean 1) excitement, or 2) movement. A fetus can stir within a womb. A penis can also stir.

"She's a dear child to me," Fabritio said.

"That must necessarily be the case," the Duke said. "You say she is your daughter."

Fabritio said:

"Nay, my good lord — dear to my purse, I mean — beside my person, I never reckoned the cost to that.

"She has the full qualities of a gentlewoman. I have brought her up to music, dancing, whatever may commend her sex and stir her husband."

"Stir" can mean 1) attract, and 2) sexually move and excite.

"And which is he now?" the Duke asked.

Referring to the Foolish Ward, who came forward, Guardiano said, "This young heir, my lord."

"What is he brought up to?" the Duke asked.

Hippolito said to himself, "To cat and trap."

The Foolish Ward and Sordido were playing earlier the game of Cat.

Trap," aka "Trap-Ball," is a similar game.

The *Oxford English Dictionary* defines "trap-ball" in this way: *"A game in which a ball, placed upon one end (slightly hollowed) of a trap [...], is thrown into the air by the batter striking the other end with his bat, with which he then hits the ball away."*

Guardiano said, "My lord, he's a great ward, wealthy, but simple."

"Simple" means "foolish."

The Duke said, "Oh, wise-acres."

The Foolish Ward was wise only in having acres. He had chosen his parents wisely: They were wealthy.

"You've described him in a word, sir," Guardiano said.

Brancha said:

"Alas, poor gentlewoman, Isabella is ill-situated, unless she's dealt with the situation more wisely and laid in more provision for her youth.

"Fools will not keep in summer."

"Provision" is resources and food.

A "fool" is a trifle with cream that will spoil in the hot summer weather.

Leantio said to himself, "No, nor such wives keep from being whores in winter."

In his opinion, wives such as Isabella would not stay loyal to their husbands.

"Yea, the voice, too, sir?" the Duke said.

He was asking if Isabella had been trained in singing.

Fabritio said:

"Aye, and it is a sweet breast, too, my lord, I hope, or I have cast away my money 'wisely.'"

The word "breast" can also mean a singing voice.

Fabritio would have cast away his money "wisely" because he had been spending in order to achieve a worthwhile goal that had not in fact been achieved.

Fabritio continued:

"She took her pricksong earlier, my lord, than any of her kindred ever did."

A "pricksong" is a song that has been pricked — written — down.

The word 'prick' can also mean "penis," and "pricksong" can mean sounds made during sex.

Fabritio continued:

"She is a splendid and talented child, though I say it; but I'd not have the baggage hear so much; it would make her swell immediately, and maidens of all things must not be puffed up."

"Baggage" can be either 1) an insult, or 2) a term of endearment.

"Swell" can mean 1) swell with pride, or 2) swell because of pregnancy.

The Duke said:

"Let's turn ourselves to a better banquet, then. For music bids the soul of man to a feast, and that's indeed a noble entertainment, worthy Brancha's self."

He then said to Brancha:

"You shall perceive, beauty, that our Florentine damsels are not brought up idly."

Brancha replied, "They are wiser of themselves — by themselves and innately — it seems, my lord, and they can take gifts when goodness offers them."

Music played.

Leantio said to himself, "True, and damnation has taught you that wisdom. You can take gifts, too. Oh, that music mocks me!"

Livia said to herself:

"I am as dumb to any language now except the language of love. Except for love-language, I am as dumb as a person is who has never learned to speak.

"I am not yet so old; he — Leantio — may still think of me romantically.

"It's my own fault, I have been idle a long time. But I'll begin the week, and paint — that is, use cosmetics — tomorrow, and so follow my true labor day by day.

"I never thrived so well as when I used it."

Her true labor may be seduction.

Isabella sang:

"What harder chance can fall to woman,

"Who was born to cleave to some man,

"Than to bestow her time, youth, beauty,

"Life's observance [a lifetime's service], honor, duty,

"On a thing [a penis] for no use good,

"But to make physic [medicine] work, or blood

"Force fresh in an old lady's cheek? She that [who] would be

"Mother of fools, let her compound [join or agree] with me."

Isabela thought that her soon-to-be-husband's penis would be of no use other than to make medicine such as laxatives work or to make an old lady blush. Such sex would be at best gentle exercise.

Because Isabella would be having sex with a fool who was her husband, she was likely to become a mother of fools.

As Isabella sang, the Foolish Ward commented on her song to himself:

"Here's a tune indeed! Bah! I had rather hear one ballad sung in the nose with a nasal tone now, about the lamentable drowning of fat sheep and oxen, than all these simpering tunes played upon cat's guts, and sung by little kitlings."

"Little kitlings" are 1) kittens, or 2) whores.

Fabritio asked the Duke, "How do you like her breast now, my lord?"

"Her breast" can mean "her voice."

Brancha said to herself, "Her breast? He talks as if his daughter had given suck before she was married, as her betters have. The next thing he praises surely will be her nipples."

Some women at court suckled their first child before the women got married.

The Duke whispered to Brancha, "I think now that such a voice, compared to such a husband, is like a jewel of invaluable — priceless — worth, hung at a fool's ear."

In this society, men wore earrings.

Fabritio asked, "May it please your grace to give her permission to demonstrate another talent?"

"By the Virgin Mary, as many good ones as you will, sir," the Duke said. "The more, the better welcome."

Leantio said to himself:

"But the fewer, the better practiced."

The fewer the kinds of art one seeks to master, the more the time and effort that can be devoted to each of them.

Leantio continued saying to himself:

"That soul's black indeed that cannot commend virtue.

"But who practices virtue?

"The extortioner will say to a sick beggar, 'May Heaven comfort thee,' although he gives no alms himself.

"This kind of 'good' is commonly practiced."

Fabritio asked Guardiano, "Will it please you now, sir, to entreat your ward to take her by the hand, and lead herein a dance before the Duke?"

Guardiano replied:

"That will I, sir; it is needful."

He then said to the Foolish Ward:

"Listen, nephew."

He whispered to him.

Fabritio said to the Foolish Ward, "You shall see, young heir, what you have for your money, without fraud or imposture."

The Foolish Ward said:

"Dance with her?

"Not I, sweet guardianer; do not urge my heart to it. It is clean against my blood — against my inclination. Dance with a stranger?

"Let whosoever will, do it. I'll not begin first with her."

Hippolito said to himself, "No, don't fear, fool. She's taken a better order: She has arranged things better."

Isabella had already taken Hippolito as her lover; to them Hippolito was a better choice of lover than the Foolish Ward.

"Why, who shall take her then?" Guardiano asked.

"Take her" can mean 1) dance with her, and/or 2) "dance" with her— that is, sleep with her.

The Foolish Ward said, "Some other gentleman. Look, there's her uncle, a fine-timbered — well-built — reveler. Perhaps he knows the manner of her dancing, too. I'll have him do it before me. I have sworn, guardianer. Then may I learn the better."

One kind of "dancing" is done in bed, but the Foolish Ward meant that he could learn to dance on the dance floor better by watching Hippolito.

"Thou shall be an ass still," Guardiano said.

The Foolish Ward replied:

"Aye, all that, uncle, shall not fool me out of my resolve. It shall not make me change my mind.

"Bah! I stick closer to myself and my wishes than that."

Guardiano said to Hippolito, "I must entreat you, sir, to take your niece and dance with her; my ward's a little willful. He would have you show him the way."

"Me, sir?" Hippolito said. "He shall command it at all hours. Please tell him so."

Yes, Hippolito was ready at all hours to "dance" with Isabella.

"I thank you for him," Guardiano said. "He has not wit and intelligence himself, sir, to thank you."

Hippolito said to Isabella:

"Come, my life's peace."

Isabella was also his piece: a woman with whom he had sex.

He said to himself:

"I have a strange office — a strange duty — of it here.

"It is some men's luck to keep the joys he likes concealed for his own bosom; but my fortune is to set the joys I like out now for another's liking."

His dancing with Isabella would display her charms to another man: the Foolish Ward.

Hippolito continued saying to himself:

"Like the mad — furious — misery of necessitous man, who parts from his good horse with many praises, and goes on foot himself."

Because the man was impoverished, he had to sell his horse, which he valued.

Hippolito continued saying to himself:

"Need and necessity must be obeyed in every action; it mars man and maiden."

Hippolito had to dance with Isabella. It was customary to dance before the Duke, and Hippolito would not disappoint him although he would be displaying Isabella to her future husband.

Music played.

Hippolito and Isabella danced, with he bowing and she curtseying to the Duke; and afterwards to each other, both before and after the dance.

The Duke said:

"Signior Fabritio, you're a happy father. Your cares and pains are fortunate, you see. Your cost bears noble fruits.

"Hippolito, thanks."

Fabritio said, "Here's some amends for all my expenses yet. She wins both prick and praise, wherever she comes."

"Prick and praise" are the best praise. A "prick" is the center of an archery target.

"How do you like it, Brancha?" the Duke asked.

"I like everything well, my lord," Brancha said. "But this poor gentlewoman's fortune, that's the worst."

"There is no doubt, Brancha, that she'll find leisure to make that good enough," the Duke said. "He's rich and simple."

Isabella could find the leisure and the opportunity to commit adultery.

"She has the better hope of the upper hand indeed, which women strive for most," Brancha said.

Guardiano said to the Foolish Ward, "Do it when I bid you, sir."

The Foolish Ward said, "I'll venture but a hornpipe with her, Guardianer, or some such married man's dance."

A "hornpipe" is a vigorous dance.

"Horns" are the emblem of a cuckold, and a "pipe" can be a penis, and so a hornpipe is a dance for a married man.

"Well, venture something, sir," Guardiano said.

"I have rhyme for what I do," the Foolish Ward said.

"But little reason, I think," Guardiano said.

The Foolish Ward recited these lines about eight kinds of dancers:

"Plain men dance the measures; the cinquepace, the gay:

"Cuckolds dance the hornpipe; and farmers dance the hay:

"Your soldiers dance the round, and maidens that [who] grow big [in pregnancy]:

"Your drunkards, the canaries; your whore and bawd, the jig."

Plain men danced the measures (a stately dance), and gay (that is, happy) men danced the cinquepace (a lively dance).

Cuckolds dance the hornpipe because of the horns.

The hay is a country dance appropriate for farmers.

Soldiers go on rounds, and pregnant maidens grow round, and so they dance the dance called the round, in which the dancers form a circle.

Drunkards danced the canaries — canary wine came from the Canary Islands — and whores and bawds danced the jig, a vigorous, lusty dance.

The Foolish Ward then said:

"Here's your eight kinds of dancers; he who finds the ninth, let him pay the minstrels."

The Duke said about the Foolish Ward, "Oh, here he appears once in his own person; I thought he would have married her by attorney, and lain with her so, too."

"By attorney" means "by proxy."

Brancha said, "Nay, my kind lord, there's very seldom any found so foolish as to give away his part there."

Leantio was not foolish, but he was being forced to allow the Duke to sleep with Brancha.

Leantio said to himself, "Bitter scoff! Yet I must do it. With what a cruel pride the glory — boastfulness — of her sin strikes by my afflictions!"

"Strikes by" may mean 1) disregards, or 2) thrusts aside.

As a result of seeing how his wife was acting, Leantio may be falling out of love with her.

Music played.

The Foolish Ward and Isabella danced, with the Foolish Ward ridiculously imitating Hippolito's dancing.

The Duke said:

"This thing will make shift — that is, struggle — sirs, to make a husband, for anything I see in him.

"What do you think, Brancha?"

Brancha said:

"Indeed, an ill-favored shift, my lord, I think."

A "shift" is an undergarment. "Ill-favored" means "stinky."

Brancha continued:

"If he would take some voyage when he's married, dangerous, or long enough, and scarcely be seen once in nine years together, a wife then might make indifferent shift to be content with him."

The Duke said, "A kiss."

He kissed her.

He then said:

"That wit deserves to be made much of.

"Come, our caroche."

A caroche is a stately coach.

Guardiano said, "It stands ready for your grace."

The Duke said to the guests:

"My thanks to all your loves."

He then said:

"Come, fair Brancha. We have taken special care of you and have provided your lodging near us now."

"Your love is great, my lord," Brancha said.

"Once more our thanks to all," the Duke said.

"All blessed honors guard you!" everyone said.

Cornets sounded.

Everyone except Leantio and Livia exited.

Without noticing Livia, Leantio said to himself:

"Have thou left me then, Brancha, utterly?

"Oh, Brancha! Now I miss thee.

"Oh! Return and save people's faith in the loyalty of Woman.

"I never felt the loss of thee until now; it is an affliction of greater weight than youth was made to bear.

"It is as if a punishment of after-life in Hell were fallen upon a man here. So new it is to flesh and blood, and so strange, so insupportable. It is a misapplied torment, as if a body whose death was meant to be drowning must necessarily therefore suffer it in scalding oil."

Livia said, "Sweet sir!"

Still not noticing Livia, Leantio continued saying to himself:

"As long as my eye saw thee, I half enjoyed thee."

Livia said, "Sir?"

Still not noticing Livia, Leantio continued saying to himself:

"Can thou forget the dear pains my love took? How it has stayed awake and watched and kept vigil whole nights together, in all weathers for thee, yet my love stood in heart merrier than the tempest that sings around my ears, like dangerous flatterers who can set all their mischief — their evil — to sweet tunes.

"And then my love received thee from thy father's window, into these arms at midnight; when we embraced as if we had been statues only made to represent love, to show art's lifelikeness, so silent were our comforts, and we kissed as if our lips had grown together. Can thou forget that?"

Livia said to herself, "This makes me madder to enjoy him now."

She wanted to enjoy him in bed.

Still not noticing Livia, Leantio continued saying to himself:

"Can thou forget all this, and better joys that we met with after this, which then new kisses took pride to celebrate and praise?"

Livia said to herself:

"I shall grow madder yet."

She then said loudly:

"Sir!"

Still not noticing Livia, Leantio continued saying to himself:

"This cannot be anything other than some secretive bawd's working."

Finally noticing Livia, he said:

"I beg your pardon, lady! What do you want to say to me?

"My sorrow makes me so unmannerly. May God's comfort bless me, I had quite forgotten you."

Livia said, "I have nothing to say, except that out of pity to that passionate grief you feel, I would give your grief good counsel and advice."

"By the Virgin Mary, it will be welcome, lady," Leantio said. "Good counsel and advice never could come at a better time."

"Then first, sir, I advise you to make away all your good thoughts at once of her," Livia said. "Know, most assuredly, that she is a strumpet."

"Huh! 'Most assuredly'?" Leantio said. "Don't speak about so vile a thing so certainly — leave it more doubtful."

"Then I must leave behind all truth," Livia said, "and not reveal my knowledge about a sin that I too lately found out about and wept for."

"Did you find it?" Leantio asked.

"Aye, with wet eyes," Livia said.

"Oh, perjurious friendship!" Leantio said.

"Perjurious friendship" described Brancha's love for Leantio, but it also can be a description of Livia's own "friendship" with Leantio's mother.

Brancha's affair with the Duke made her wedding vows to Leantio perjurious.

Livia's professed vows of friendship to Leantio's mother were also perjurious.

Livia said:

"You missed your fortunes when you met with her, sir.

"Young gentlemen, who love only for beauty, do not love wisely; such a marriage rather proves to be the destruction of affection.

"It brings on want and poverty, which are the key to whoredom.

"I think you'd had small means — a small dowry — with her?"

"Oh, not any, lady," Leantio said.

They had eloped, and so there was no dowry.

Livia said:

"Alas, poor gentleman! What do thou mean, sir, quite to undo — to ruin — thyself with thine own kind heart?"

By marrying Brancha for love, Leantio had deprived himself of a good dowry. At best, her "dowry" had been whatever possessions Brancha could grab before leaving the house when she eloped.

Livia continued:

"Thou are too good and pitiful to Woman.

"By the Virgin Mary, sir, thank thy stars for this blessed fortune that rids the summer of thy youth so well from many beggars, who had else only lain sunning in thy beams, until thou had wasted the whole days of thy life in heat and labor."

If Leantio had received a substantial dowry, he may have been pursued by many gold-diggers who were not his wife. He has been spared that.

Also, Brancha's adultery has spared him from having many children — beggars — to support with labor since he has received no dowry.

The "heat and labor" could be sexual heat and labor, or it can be hard work.

Livia continued:

"What would you say now to a creature found as full of pity for you, and as it were even sent on purpose from the whole female sex in general, to requite all that kindness you have shown to it?"

"Who's that, madam?" Leantio asked.

Livia replied:

"A gentlewoman, and one able to reward good things; aye, and one who bears a conscience to it.

Livia was offering to do something in good conscience: something she could do without feeling guilt. In fact, she was saying that she considered it a duty to help Leantio.

Livia continued:

"Could thou love such a one, who — blow, all fortunes, good and/or bad; let fate take its course — would never see thee lack anything?

"Nay, more, this person would maintain thee in such a way that thine enemy will envy thee, and thou shall not spend a care for it, shall not stir a thought, and shall not break a sleep — unless love's music awakened thee. No storm of fortune would wake thee.

"Look upon me and know the woman who will do this for thee."

Leantio said, "Oh, my life's wealth, Brancha!"

Livia said to herself:

"Still with her name? Will nothing wear it out?"

She then said to Leantio:

"That deep sigh went for only a strumpet, sir."

Leantio said, "It can go for no other woman who loves me."

Livia said to herself:

"He's vexed in his mind. I came too soon to him.

"Where's my discretion now, my skill, my judgment? I'm cunning in all arts except my own love."

Livia was talented at arranging love affairs for other people, but she regretted that she was now not successful at arranging a love affair with Leantio for herself.

Livia continued saying to herself:

"It is as unseasonable to tempt him now so soon, as for a widow to be courted following her husband's corpse; or to make a bargain — a marriage engagement — by the graveside and take a young man there.

"Brancha's strange, not-yet-familiar departure stands like a hearse yet before his eyes; time will take it down shortly.

A hearse was a wooden ornamental structure displayed during funerals and for a while afterward in the deceased's church.

The hearse will be taken down later, and the memory of the deceased will also be taken down — that is, lessened.

Livia exited.

Alone, Leantio said to himself:

"Is she my wife until death, yet no more mine?

"That's a hard measure.

"Then what's marriage good for?

"I think by right I should not now be living, and then it would all be well. What a happiness would I have had if I had never seen her!

"For nothing makes man's loss grievous to him, but knowledge of the worth of what he loses. For what he never had, he never misses."

"She's gone forever, utterly; there is as much redemption of a soul from Hell, as a beautiful woman's body from the Duke's palace."

The damned in Hell are tormented by the knowledge of what they have lost: They will never reside in Heaven.

According to medieval theology, with the exception of Jesus' Harrowing of Hell after His death on the cross, the souls of those in Hell will never be redeemed.

In Dante's *Inferno*, these words are written above the entrance to Hell: ABANDON ALL HOPE, ALL YE WHO ENTER.

Leantio continued saying to himself:

"Why should my love last longer than her truth: her loyalty to our marriage vows?

"What is there good in Woman to be loved, when only that which makes her so has left her?

"I cannot love her now, unless I must accept her sin, and my own shame, too, and be guilty of consenting to her law's breach — her adultery — and my own abusing, all of which would be monstrous!

"So then my safest course for health of mind and body is to turn my heart, and hate her, most extremely hate her.

"I have no other way. Those virtuous Powers that were chaste witnesses of both our troths — our wedding vows — can witness she breaks them first!"

Powers are one of the nine orders of angels:

The Seraphim, Cherubim, and Thrones.

The Dominations, Virtues, and Powers.

The Principalities, Archangels, and Angels.

Leantio continued saying to himself:

"And I'm rewarded with the captainship of the fort. It is a position of prestige, I must confess, but it is poor in financial rewards. My factorship shall not exchange means with it — my job as a merchant's agent is just as financially rewarding.

"The most recent Captain of that citadel was no drunkard, yet he died a beggar, despite all his thrift; besides, the place does not fit me. It suits my resolution, not my breeding: It suits my courage, but not my birth."

Leantio was brought up to be a merchant's agent, not a soldier.

Livia returned.

She said to herself:

"I have tried all the ways I can, and I have not the power to keep away from the sight of him."

She said out loud to Leantio:

"How are you now, sir?"

"I feel a better ease, madam," Leantio answered.

Livia said:

"Thanks be to God's blessedness!

"You will do well, I promise you; don't fear, sir.

"Just join your own good will to it.

"He's not wise who loves his pain or sickness, or grows fond of a disease, whose symptom is to vex him, and spitefully drink his blood up. A curse upon it, sir! Youth knows no greater loss than unrequited love.

"I ask that we walk, sir.

"You never saw the beauty of my house yet, nor how abundantly fortune has blessed me in worldly treasure."

Matthew 6:19-21 (King James Version) states:

19) Lay not up for yourselves treasures upon earth, where moth and rust doth corrupt, and where thieves break through and steal:

20) But lay up for yourselves treasures in heaven, where neither moth nor rust doth corrupt, and where thieves do not break through nor steal:

21) For where your treasure is, there will your heart be also.

Livia continued:

"Trust me that I have enough, sir, to make my friend — that is, my lover — a rich man in my life, a great man at my death; you yourself will say so.

"If you want anything, and spare to speak — that is, don't ask for it — then truly, I'll condemn you for a willful man, sir."

"Why, surely this can only be the flattery of some dream," Leantio said.

Livia said:

"Now, by this kiss, my love, my soul, and my riches, it is all true substance!

"It is all real!"

She kissed him.

She continued:

"Come, you shall see my wealth; take what you wish.

"The gallanter and more fashionably you dress and go about, the more you please me. I will allow you, too, your page and footman, your racehorses, or any of the various pleasures that exercised youth — young people who engage in sports — delight in.

"But only to me, sir, wear your heart of constant stuff."

"Constant clothing" does not change color. Here, Livia was telling Leantio to be constant and faithful to her. That meant not being constant and faithful to Brancha.

Livia continued:

"If you will only love me enough, I'll give you enough."

Leantio said, "Truly, then, I'll love enough, and take enough."

"Then we are both pleased enough," Livia said.

They exited.

Guardiano and Isabella entered a room at one door, and the Foolish Ward and Sordido entered the room at another door.

Guardiano said to the Foolish Ward, "Now, nephew, here's the gentlewoman again."

"By the Mass!" the Foolish Ward said. "Here she's come again! Look at her now, Sordido."

Guardiano said:

"This is the maiden whom my love and care has chosen for your wife, and so I tender her to you. You yourself have been eyewitness of some qualities that bespeak a courtly breeding and are costly to acquire.

"I bring you both to talk together now. It is time you grew familiar in your tongues and engaged in conversation.

"Tomorrow, you join hands, and one ring ties you, and one bed holds you; if you like the choice, her father and her friends and relatives are in the next room, and they stay to see the marriage contract before they depart.

"Therefore, dispatch and be quick, good ward, be sweet and short.

"Like her, or like her not, there's but two ways.

"And one your body, the other your purse pays."

If the Foolish Ward marries, he pays with his body.

If the Foolish Ward does not marry, he pays his guardian a fine.

"I promise you, guardianer," the Foolish Ward said, "I'll not stand all day thrumming, but quickly shoot my bolt at your next coming."

"Thrumming means 1) idly or unskillfully strumming a musical instrument, or 2) having sex.

"Shoot my bolt" means 1) tell you my decision, or 2) ejaculate.

A proverb stated, "A fool's bolt is soon shot."

The bolt is literally an arrow and figuratively a penis.

The proverb could be restated in this way: A fool's penis prematurely ejaculates.

Guardiano replied, "Well said. Good fortune to your birding then."

"Birding" means 1) hunting birds, or 2) chasing women.

Guardiano exited.

"I never missed the mark yet," the Foolish Ward said.

A mark is 1) a target, or 2) a vagina.

Sordido said, "Indeed, I think, master, if the truth were known, you never shot at any but the kitchen-wench, and she was a she-woodcock, a mere innocent [half-wit], who was often lost and cried at eight-and-twenty."

Woodcocks are birds that are proverbially stupid.

When a child was lost, the town crier would announce the news and people would look for the child. When the child was found, the town crier would announce that fact.

The Foolish Ward said:

"No more of that meat, Sordido. Here's eggs on the spit now."

Eggs could be cooked on a spit, but the cook had to be watchful while cooking them.

The Foolish Ward continued:

"We must turn gingerly; we must draw out the catalog of all the faults of women."

Sordido said:

"What! All the faults? Have you so little reason that you think so much paper will fit in my breeches?"

Writing down Isabella's faults would take a lot of paper.

Sordido continued:

"Why, ten carts will not carry it, even if you set down only the bawds."

A common punishment for bawds and prostitutes was to be put on a cart and carted through the streets.

Sordido continued:

"All the faults? Please, let's be content with a few of them; and if they were less, you would find them enough, I guarantee you.

"Look, sir."

Aware that the Foolish Ward was judging her, Isabella said to herself:

"Except that I have the advantage of the fool and have the ability to outwit and manipulate him, as much as a woman's heart can wish and joy at, what an infernal torment it would be to be thus bought and sold, and turned and pried into, when, alas, the worst bit of me is too good for him! The comfort is that he has only a cater's place on it, and he provides all for another's table."

A cater is a person who buys the provisions for a household. Cates are delicacies.

Isabella continued saying to herself:

"Yet how curious and fastidious in his inspection of me the ass is; he is like some nice professor — some pedantic professed expert — on it, who buys up all the daintiest food in the markets, and seldom licks his lips after a taste of it."

Perhaps we need a proverb that states, "He is an ill cater who cannot lick his own lips."

Metaphorically, Isabella was saying that the Foolish Ward was closely scrutinizing her sexiness but would seldom have sex with her after the first time.

Sordido said, "Now go to her, now that you've scanned all her parts over."

"But at which end shall I begin now, Sordido?" the Foolish Ward asked.

"Oh, always at a woman's lip, while you live, sir," Sordido said. "Do you really need to ask that question?"

Yes. Which lip? A woman has lips at both ends: top and bottom.

The Foolish Ward said, "I think, Sordido, she's only a crabbed face to begin with."

"A crabbed face?" Sordido said. "That will save money."

"What!" the Foolish Ward said. "How will it save money, Sordido?"

Sordido said:

"Aye, sir; because she has a crabbed face of her own, she'll eat the less verjuice with her mutton."

Verjuice is a sour sauce made from crab-apples.

Sordido continued:

"It will save verjuice at year's end, sir."

The Foolish Ward said, "Nay, if your jests begin to be saucy now, I'll make you eat your meat without mustard."

"And that in some kind is a punishment," Sordido said.

A tale was told about a man who when he was in danger vowed to stop eating meat if his life were saved, but when the danger considerably lessened, he changed the vow to not eating meat with mustard if his life were saved.

The Foolish Ward went over to Isabella and said:

"Gentlewoman, they say it is your pleasure to be my wife, and you shall know shortly whether it is my pleasure or not to be your husband, and thereupon thus I first enter upon — encounter — you."

He kissed her and then said:

"Oh, most delicious scent! I think it tasted as if a man had stepped into a comfit-maker's shop to let a cart go by, all the while I kissed her."

A comfit-maker is a confectioner. His shop would smell good.

The Foolish Ward continued:

"It is reported, gentlewoman, you'll run mad for me if you don't have me."

Isabella said:

"I should be in great danger of my wits, sir, for being so forward —"

She then said to herself:

"— should this ass kick backward and refuse to marry now."

"Forward" means "straightforward," but Isabella also used it with the meaning of getting close to an ass and being in danger of getting kicked.

The Foolish Ward said:

"Alas, poor soul!

"And is that hair your own?"

Baldness was a sign of venereal disease. Some people suffering from venereal disease wore a wig.

Isabella said, "My own? Yes, it is sure, sir, that I owe nothing for it."

In Thomas Middleton's day, boys played the roles of women on stage. The boy playing the role of Isabella would be wearing a wig.

The Foolish Ward replied:

"It is good to hear that. I shall have the less to pay when I have married you."

He then said to Sordido:

"Look, do her eyes stand well? Are they well-placed?"

"They cannot stand better than in her head, I think," Sordido said. "Where would you have them? And as for her nose, it is of a very good last."

Cobblers used lasts to shape shoes.

"I have known a nose as good as hers that has not lasted a year, though," the Foolish Ward said.

Sordido said, "That's in the using of a thing; wouldn't any strong bridge fall down in time, if we do nothing but beat at the bottom? A nose of buff — that is, strong leather — would not last always, sir, especially if it came into the military camp once."

People who suffered from syphilis sometimes had a collapsed nose.

Prostitutes were numerous around a military camp, and many soldiers suffered from venereal disease.

The Foolish Ward said, "But, Sordido, what shall we do to make her laugh, so that I may see what teeth she has, for I'll not bate her a tooth, nor take a black one into the bargain."

He would marry Isabella only if she had a full set of white teeth.

"Why, just fall in talk with her," Sordido said. "You cannot choose but one time or other to make her laugh, sir."

The Foolish Ward was sure to say something foolish that would make Isabella laugh.

The Foolish Ward said:

"It shall go hard, but I will make her laugh."

He said to Isabella:

"Please tell me what qualities you have besides singing and dancing. Can you play at shittlecock, truly?"

Isabella replied, "Aye, and at stool-ball too, sir; I have great luck at it."

Stool-ball is a game like cricket; the wicket is a stool.

"Why, can you catch a ball well?" the Foolish Ward asked.

Isabella said, "I have caught two in my lap at one game."

Hmm. Two balls in her lap? The balls belonged to Hippolito, and he had shared them with Isabella.

One "game" is one bout of sex.

"What!" the Foolish Ward said. "Have you, woman? I must have you learn to play at trap, too, and then you're full and whole."

Hmm. "Full" and "hole." Say no more.

Isabella said, "Anything that you please to bring me up to, I shall take pains to practice."

Hmm. A "thing" can be a penis. Isabella is willing to practice on any thing to maintain proficiency in a certain activity.

The Foolish Ward said, "It will not do, Sordido. We shall never get her mouth open wide enough."

Sordido said:

"No, sir? That's strange! Then here's a trick for your learning."

Sordido yawned and then said:

"Look now! Look now! Quick! Quick there!"

Isabella yawned, also, but she covered her mouth with a handkerchief.

The Foolish Ward said, "A pox on that scurvy mannerly — polite — trick with her handkerchief. It hindered me a little, but I am satisfied. When a fair woman yawns, and stops her mouth so, it looks like a cloth stopper in a cream-pot. I have fair hope of her teeth now, Sordido."

Cream is white, and so may be Isabella's teeth.

Sordido said:

"Why then you've all well, sir, for ought I see.

"She's right and straight enough, now as she stands. They'll commonly lie crooked, but that doesn't matter."

In other words: When she lies down for sex, she does not lie straight. Her knees are in the air.

Sordido continued:

"Wise gamesters — pursuers of sex — never find fault with that. Let them lie always like that."

The Foolish Ward said:

"I'd like to see how she walks, and then I have learned all I need to make my decision, for of all creatures I cannot abide a splay-footed woman: a woman who walks with her feet turned out. She's an unlucky thing to meet in a morning; her heels keep together so, as if she were beginning an Irish dance always, and the wriggling of her bum were playing the tune to it.

"But I have thought of a cleanly shift — a neat trick — to find it. Duck down as you see me do, and peep on one side, when her back's toward you; I'll show you the way."

Sordido said, "And you shall find me apt enough to peeping. I have been one of them who has seen mad sights under your scaffolds."

Scaffolds were platforms; plays were sometimes performed on them. Sordido sometimes peeped up the dresses of ladies on the scaffold.

The Foolish Ward said to Isabella, "Will it please you to walk, truly, a turn or two by yourself? You are so pleasing to me that I take delight in viewing you on both sides."

Isabella replied:

"I shall be glad to fetch a walk to please your love for me, sir. It will get affection a good stomach, sir."

"Stomach" means "appetite." It can mean "sexual appetite."

She then said to herself:

"I must have a good stomach to fall to such coarse victuals."

The coarse victuals were the Foolish Ward and his performance in bed.

Isabella walked to the end of the stage, and the Foolish Ward and Sordido stooped down to try to look under her skirt.

The Foolish Ward said, "Now go thy ways — off you go — for a clean treading wench, as any man in modesty peeped under."

"Clean-treading" means "straight-walking," but "to tread" can also mean "to have sex."

Sordido said, "I see the sweetest sight to please my master. Never went a Frenchman righter upon tightropes than she walks on Florentine rushes."

Rushes were used as a covering for floors.

"It is enough, indeed," the Foolish Ward said.

Isabella asked, "And how do you like me now, sir?"

The Foolish Ward said, "Truly, I like you so well that I never mean to part with thee, sweetheart, before we have some sixteen children, and all boys."

Isabella said, "You'll be at simple pains, if you prove to be true to type, and you will breed them all in your teeth."

"Simple pains" are the pains of a fool. "Simple pains" can also be great pains.

This society believed that when a woman was in labor, her husband would sometimes suffer toothaches as a form of sympathetic pain.

If the Foolish Ward were to breed children with his teeth and not with his penis, all of his children would be bastards.

The Foolish Ward said, "Nay, by my faith, what does your belly serve for? It would make my cheeks look like blown bagpipes."

Guardiano entered the scene.

He asked, "How are you two now, ward and nephew, gentlewoman and niece! Speak, is it so or not? Is it a marriage or not?"

"It is so," the Foolish Ward said. "We are both agreed to be married, sir."

"Go inside to your kindred then," Guardiano said. "There's friends, and wine, and music waiting to welcome you."

The Foolish Ward said, "Then I'll be drunk for joy."

"And I'll be drunk for company," Sordido said. "I cannot break my nose in a better action — I cannot suffer in a better cause."

Sordido's nose would become red from the wine he drank.

The word "nose" sometimes meant "penis." Alcohol can inflame desire but take away performance.

They exited.

CHAPTER 4

— 4.1 —

Brancha, attended by two ladies, entered a room of Brancha's lodgings near the court.

"How go your watches, ladies?" Brancha asked. "What time is it now?"

In this society, cynics said that clocks and watches and women were often false. The clocks and watches often showed the wrong time, and the ladies had sex with men who were not their husbands and so they were not true to their husbands.

"By my watch, it is full nine," the first lady said.

"By my watch, it is a quarter past," the second lady said.

"I set my watch by St. Mark's Church," the first lady said.

"They say St. Anthony's Church goes truer," the second lady said.

"That's just your opinion, madam, because you love a gentleman of the name," the first lady said.

"He's a true gentleman then," the second lady said.

"So may he be who comes to me tonight, for ought you know," the first lady said.

Brancha said, "I'll end this strife straightaway. I set my watch by the sun; I love to set by the best, because one shall not then be troubled to set often."

The sun often represented the ruler. Here it represents the Duke of Florence, with whom Brancha was sleeping.

In this conversation, "setting the watch" figuratively means "sleeping with a man."

The Duke of Florence may be good in bed, and so Brancha may not need to have a lot of sex with him to be sexually satisfied. And her libido may be low.

Or perhaps he is bad at sex, and Brancha prefers not to have much sex with him.

"You do wisely in it," the second lady said.

Brancha said:

"If I should set my watch as some girls do by every clock in the town, it would never go true."

Women who set their watch by every clock in the town are promiscuous.

Brancha continued:

"And too much turning of the dial's point, or tampering with the spring, might in a short time spoil the whole work, too."

Hmm. The "dial's point" is the tip of a penis, and the "spring" is the *mons veneris*. Push down on the fatty layer, remove your hand, and it will spring back. Same with pushing down on the tip of an erect penis.

Brancha continued:

"Here by my watch, it is approaching nine now."

"It does indeed, truly," the first lady said. "Mine's nearest the truth yet."

"Yet I have found her lying with an advocate, which looked like two false clocks together in one parish," the second lady said.

Advocates are lawyers who may lie professionally. The first lady is "false" in the sense that she is having an affair.

"So now I thank you, ladies," Brancha said. "I desire for a while to be alone."

The first lady said:

"And I am nobody, I think, unless I have some person or other with me."

She then said to herself:

"Indeed, my desire and hers — Brancha's — will never be sisters."

The first lady and the second lady exited.

Alone, Brancha said to herself:

"How strangely Woman's fortune comes about!

"This was the farthest way for my fortune to come to me, all would have judged, who knew me born in Venice, and there with many suspicious eyes brought up, who never thought they had me sure enough except when the suspicious eyes were upon me, yet my fate is to meet it here, so far off from my birthplace, my friends, and my kindred.

"It is not good, seriously, to keep a maiden so strict in her young days. Restraint breeds wandering thoughts, as many fasting days breed a great desire to see flesh stirring again."

"Flesh stirring" can mean 1) meat becoming available again, or 2) a penis becoming erect.

Brancha continued saying to herself:

"I'll never treat any girl of mine so strictly. However they're kept, their fortunes find them out. I see it in myself. If they are begotten in court, I'll never forbid them the country; nor will I forbid them the court, although they were born in the country.

"They will come to it, and they will go a thousand miles out of their way to fall into sin, where one would little expect it would happen."

Leantio, who was richly dressed, entered the scene.

Leantio said:

"I long to see how my despiser looks, now that she's come here to court: These are her lodgings. She's absolutely now advanced."

He looked at a window and said:

"I took her out of no such window. I remember when we first met. That was a great deal lower, and less carved."

Brancha said, "How are things now! What silkworm — fancy dresser — is this? In the name of pride! What! Is it he?"

Leantio said, "A bow in the ham to your greatness. You must have now three legs, I take it, mustn't you?"

"Three legs" can mean 1) three bows, or 2) three penises. Or it can mean Brancha's two legs and the Duke's penis.

Brancha said:

"Then I must take another; I shall lack otherwise the service I should have."

"Service" can mean "sexual service" as well as "deference."

Brancha continued:

"You have but two there."

Leantio had two legs.

"You're richly placed," Leantio said.

"I think you're wondrously well-dressed, sir," Brancha said.

"A sumptuous lodging," Leantio said.

"You've an excellent suit of clothing there," Brancha said.

"A chair of velvet," Leantio said.

"Does your cloak have a lining throughout, sir?" Brancha asked.

Expensive cloaks had that feature.

"You're very stately here," Leantio said.

"Indeed, something proud and splendid, sir," Brancha said.

"Wait, wait, let's see your cloth of silver slippers," Leantio said.

"Cloth of silver" was cloth that had silver threads woven in it.

"Who's your shoemaker?" Brancha said. "He's made you a neat boot."

A "boot" can be something given to make up a deficiency. Leantio had lost Brancha, but now he had fine boots and fine clothing.

"Will you have a pair?" Leantio said. "The Duke will lend you a pair of spurs."

The Duke could spur her on in bed with his pair of testicles.

"Yes," Brancha said, "when I ride."

The riding could be done on a horse or in bed.

"It is a brave life you lead," Leantio said.

"I could never see you in such good clothes in my time," Brancha said.

"In your time?" Leantio asked.

"Surely, I think, sir, we both thrive best asunder," Brancha said.

"You're a whore," Leantio said.

"Fear nothing, sir," Brancha said. "Don't worry about it."

"You're an impudent, spiteful strumpet," Leantio said.

"Oh, sir, you give me thanks for your captainship," Brancha said. "I thought you had forgotten all your good manners."

Leantio said:

"And, to spite thee as much, look there; there read."

He gave her a letter.

Leantio continued:

"Gnaw your lip in vexation; thou shall find there I am not love-starved. The world was never yet so cold, or pitiless, but there was always still more charity found out than at one proud fool's door; and it would be hard, indeed, if I could not pass by and surpass that.

"Read to thy shame there. She is a cheerful and a beauteous benefactor, too, as ever erected the good works of love."

The erection could be the creation of a charitable institution, or the erection of a penis.

Looking at the letter, Brancha said to herself:

"Lady Livia! Is it possible? Her worship was my pandress.

"She dotes, and sends, and gives, and all to him!

"Why, here's a bawd-plagued home!"

The bawd — Livia — was herself plagued with love.

Brancha then said to her legitimate husband, Leantio:

"You're entirely happy, sir, yet I'll not envy you."

"No, court-saint, not thou," Leantio said. "You keep some friend — some lover — of a new fashion. There's no harm in your devil; he's a suckling. But he will breed teeth shortly, won't he?"

In other words: Leantio was comparing Brancha to a witch and the Duke to a familiar spirit that she was suckling. Soon, the Duke will show his teeth.

"Take heed you don't play then too long with him," Brancha said.

Leantio said:

"Yes, and the great one, too."

The "great one" is 1) the Duke, and/or 2) the Devil.

Leantio continued:

"I shall find time to play a hot religious bout with some of you, and perhaps drive you and your course of sins to their eternal kennels."

A "course" is a "pack," as of dogs.

Leantio was threatening to kill Brancha and the Duke, but not now.

Leantio continued:

"I speak softly now; it is good manners to speak softly in a noble woman's lodgings, and I well know all my degrees of duty.

"But if I should come to your everlasting parting — your deathbed — once, thunder shall seem soft music to that tempest."

Brancha said, "It was said last week there would be a change of weather, when the moon hung so, and perhaps you heard it."

Brancha may have made the signs of horns on her head when she mentioned the moon, thus saying that it was a horned — crescent — moon and that Leantio was a cuckold.

Leantio said:

"Why here's sin made, and a conscience that is never troubled; here's a monster with all forehead — impudence — and no eyes!

"Why do I talk to thee about sense or virtue, thou who are as dark as death?

"It is as much madness to set light before thee, as if to lead blind folks to see the monuments, which they may smell as soon as they behold."

Monuments are statues.

Leantio continued:

"By the Virgin Mary, often their heads, for lack of light, may feel the hardness of the monuments when they hit their heads on the monuments.

"So shall thy blind pride feel my revenge and anger.

"Thy blind pride cannot see it now; and it may fall on thee at such an hour when thou least see of all.

"So to an ignorance darker than thy womb, I leave thy perjured soul — a plague will come!"

Brancha's soul was perjured because she had violated her wedding vows.

Leantio exited.

As he exited, Brancha said:

"Get you gone first, and then I fear no greater plague than you."

Alone, Brancha said to herself about Leantio:

"Nor will I fear thee long: I'll have this sauciness soon banished from these lodgings, and the rooms perfumed well after the corrupt air leaves it.

"His breath has made me almost sick, truly.

"A poor base upstart! On God's life! Because he has gotten fair clothes by foul means, he comes to complain and criticize me, and to show off his clothes."

The Duke, who had seen Leantio leaving, entered the scene and asked, "Who's that?"

"I beg your mercy, sir!" Brancha said.

"Please tell me who's that," the Duke said.

"The former thing, my lord, to whom you gave the captainship," Brancha said. "He still eats his food with grudging."

"Still!" the Duke said.

He was used to bribing people who stayed bribed.

"He comes vaunting — boasting — here of his new love, and the new clothes she gave him: Lady Livia," Brancha said. "Who but she is now his mistress?"

"Lady Livia?" the Duke said. "Be sure of what you say. Be sure that it is true."

Brancha said, "He showed me her name, sir, in perfumed paper, her vows, her letter, with an intent to spite me. So his heart said, and his threats made it good; they were as spiteful as ever malice uttered, and as dangerous, should his hand follow the copy."

In other words: If Leantio did what he said he would do, he would become violent.

Schoolboys copied passages of writing into their copybooks.

"But that must not be," the Duke said. "Do not vex your mind; please go to bed; go. All shall be well and quiet."

"I love peace, sir," Brancha said.

She exited.

Alone, the Duke said to himself:

"And so do all who love. Take you no worry for it. It shall be still provided to you as you wish."

He then called for a servant:

"Who's near us there?"

A messenger entered the scene and said, "My lord."

The Duke ordered, "Seek out Hippolito, brother to Lady Livia, with all speed."

"He was the last man I saw, my lord," the messenger said.

"The Duke said:

"Make haste."

The messenger exited.

Alone, the Duke said to himself:

"He is a blood soon stirred — a young man easily aroused to anger — and as he's quick to apprehend a wrong, he's bold, and he's sudden and impetuous in bringing forth a ruinous result. I know likewise that the reputation of his sister's honor is as dear to him as lifeblood to his heart.

"Besides, I'll flatter him with a goodness — a benefit — to her, which I previously thought about, but never meant to practice, because I know that she is morally base."

Livia has played the role of a bawd for the Duke.

The Duke continued saying to himself:

"That wind drives him."

The Duke knew how to manipulate Hippolito.

The Duke continued saying to himself:

"The ulcerous reputation feels the weight of the lightest wrongs, just as sores are vexed with flies."

In other words: People with bad reputations feel much pain from even the slightest wrongs done to them.

Hippolito entered the scene.

The Duke said to himself:

"He comes."

He then said:

"Hippolito, welcome."

"My loved lord," Hippolito said.

The Duke asked:

"How is that lusty — that lively — widow, thy kind sister doing? Isn't she yet furnished with a second husband?"

Actually, Livia has been widowed twice, so her next husband would be her third husband.

The Duke continued:

"A bedfellow she has; I don't ask about that. I know she's enjoyed him in bed. "

Hippolito said, "You ask about him, my lord?"

"Yes, about a bedfellow," the Duke said. "Is the news so strange to you?"

"I hope it is so strange to all," Hippolito said.

He did not want Livia, his sister, to get a bad reputation.

The Duke said:

"I wish it were, sir, but her behavior has confessed too quickly and obviously that her ignorant pleasures, instructed only by lust, have received into their services an impudent boaster: one who raises his glory from her shame, and tells the midday sun what's done in darkness."

Leantio had raised his glory by using Livia's wealth to buy new, expensive clothing and to live well.

The Duke continued:

"Yet, blinded with her sexual appetite, she wastes her wealth and buys her disgraces at a dearer rate than bounteous housekeepers spend to buy a good reputation for their hospitality.

"Nothing saddens me so much as that in love to thee and to thy family, I had picked out a worthy match for her, the great Vincentio, who is high in our favor and in all men's thoughts."

"Oh, thou destruction of all happy fortunes, insatiable sexual desire!" Hippolito said. "Do you know the name, my lord, of her abuser?"

"One Leantio," the Duke said.

"He's a factor," Hippolito said.

A factor is a commercial agent — a merchant's agent or clerk. Leantio's social class was lower than that of Hippolito and Livia.

The Duke said, "He never made so splendid a voyage, according to what he says."

The splendid voyage is 1) a commercial trip, and/or 2) sex with Livia.

"He's the poor old widow's son!" Hippolito said. "I humbly take my leave."

The Duke said to himself:

"I see it is done."

He had succeeded in manipulating Hippolito.

The Duke then said out loud about Livia:

"Give her good counsel and make her see her error. I know she'll listen to you."

Hippolito said:

"Yes, my lord, I don't doubt, as I shall take a course of action that she shall never know about until it is enacted. And when she wakes to honor, then she'll thank me for it.

"I'll imitate the pities of old surgeons to this lost limb; who, before they show their art, cast one asleep, and then cut the diseased part."

The "limb" Livia will lose will be 1) her bad reputation, and 2) Leantio and his penis.

The "old surgeons" used an early form of anesthesia: sponges soaked with a narcotic.

Hippolito continued:

"So out of love to her I pity most, she shall not feel him going until he's lost. Then she'll commend the cure."

He exited.

The Duke said:

"The great cure's past; I count this done already; his wrath's sure, and it promises a deep injury.

"Farewell, Leantio. This place will never hear thee murmur more."

The Duke was sure that Hippolito would kill Leantio, who was sleeping with Hippolito's sister.

Leantio wanted to kill the Duke, who was sleeping with Leantio's wife.

The Lord Cardinal, who was the Duke's brother, entered the scene. A few attendants were with him.

The Duke said:

"Our noble brother, welcome!"

The Lord Cardinal told his attendants:

"Set those lights down."

The attendants set down the lights, which were literally candles.

The Lord Cardinal was bringing literal and symbolic light into the darkness of a sinful court.

The Lord Cardinal then told his attendants:

"Depart until you are called."

The attendants exited.

The Duke said to himself:

"There's serious business fixed in his look; nay, it inclines a little to the dark color of a discontentment."

He then asked out loud:

"Brother, what is it that commands your eye so powerfully?

"Speak, you seem lost in thought."

The Lord Cardinal said, "The thing I look at seems lost — lost forever to my eyes."

"You look at me," the Duke said.

The Lord Cardinal said, "What a grief it is to a religious feeling, to think a man should have a friend so splendid, so wise, so noble, nay, a duke, a brother, and all this certainly damned!"

"What!" the Duke said.

Damnation is for the little people. So thought the Duke.

He was not accustomed to anyone telling him that he was damned.

The Lord Cardinal said:

"It is no wonder that you are damned, if your great sin can do it.

"Do you dare to look up without thinking of a divine vengeance? Do you dare to sleep for fear of never waking, except to wake up to death? And do you dedicate to a strumpet's love the strength of your affections, zeal and energy, and health?

"Here you stand now. Can you assure your pleasures that you shall once more enjoy her? Just once more?

"Alas! You cannot. What a misery it is then to be more certain of eternal death than of a next embrace!

"Shall I show you how more unfortunate you stand in sin than the low, private, politically insignificant man?

"All his offences, like enclosed, fenced-off grounds, keep only about himself, and seldom stretch beyond his own soul's bounds.

"And when a man grows miserable, it is some comfort when he's no further charged and burdened than with his own sins. It is a sweet ease to wretchedness.

"But, great man, every sin thou commit shows like a flame — a signal beacon — upon a mountain; it is seen far away. And with a big wind made of popular breath — gossip by the common people, the sparkles fly through cities. Here one takes fire, another catches fire there, and in a short time they waste all to cinders.

"But remember always that what burnt the valleys first came from the hill. Every offence brings with it its appropriate and particular pain, but it is being an example that proves to be the great man's poison.

"The sins of mean men lie like scattered parcels of an imperfect bill — like separate items of a bill that has not been totaled up, but when great men fall, then comes example, and that sums up all."

Great men are judged more harshly than common men because great men serve as examples for other men to follow. If great men violate the law with impunity, so will lesser men.

The Duke engaged in unethical sex, and Hippolito engaged in unethical sex.

The Duke was willing to arrange for Leantio's murder, and Hippolito was willing to murder Leantio.

The Duke raped Brancha, and that rape will result in many deaths.

The Lord Cardinal continued:

"And this your reason grants:

"If men of good lives who by their virtuous actions stir up others to noble and religious imitation, receive the greater glory after death — as sin must necessarily confess — what may great sinners feel in height of torments, and in weight of vengeance — not only they themselves, not doing well — but set a light up to show men to Hell?"

"If you have finished, I have," the Duke said. "No more, sweet brother."

The Lord Cardinal said:

"I know time spent in goodness is too tedious. This had not been a moment's space in lust now."

In other words: Listening to talk about goodness is tedious and passes slowly. The same amount of time spent in having sex would seem like a moment.

The Lord Cardinal continued:

"How dare you venture on eternal pain, who cannot bear a minute's reprehension and rebuke?

"I think you should endure to hear that talked of which you so strive to suffer.

"Oh, my brother, what would you be if you were taken by death now!

"My heart weeps blood to think about it; it is a deed of infinite mercy — a deed that you can never merit and deserve — that so far you are not death-struck. No, not yet."

"I dare not delay you long, for fear you would not have time enough allowed you to repent in.

"There's only this wall" — he pointed to the Duke's body — "between you and destruction, when you're at your strongest; and it is only poor thin clay.

"Think upon it, brother. Can you come so near destruction, for a fair strumpet's love? And can you fall into a torment that knows neither end nor bottom, for beauty, just the deepness of a skin, and that not of their own either, being merely the result of cosmetics?

"Is she a thing whom sickness dare not visit, or age look on, or death resist? Does the worm shun her grave?"

A perfect soul is immutable and not subject to illness, old age, and death.

The Lord Cardinal continued:

"If the worm does not shun her grave — as your soul knows — why should lust bring man to lasting pain for rotten dust?"

The Book of Common Prayer contains these words: "*We therefore commit this body to the ground, earth to earth, ashes to ashes, dust to dust; in sure and certain hope of the Resurrection to eternal life.*"

The Duke said:

"Brother of spotless honor, let me weep the first of my repentance in thy bosom, and show the blessed fruits of a thankful spirit.

"And if I ever keep a woman, unlawfully, anymore, may I lack penitence at my greatest need. And wise men know there is no barren place that threatens more famine, than a dearth in grace."

The Lord Cardinal said:

"Why, here's a conversion that is at this time, brother, sung for a hymn in Heaven, and at this instant the powers of darkness groan, and all Hell is made sorry."

Luke 15:10 states, "*Likewise, I say unto you, there is joy in the presence of the angels of God over one sinner that repenteth*" (King James Version).

The Lord Cardinal continued:

"First, I praise heaven, then in my work I glory."

He then called for an attendant:

"Who's attending there outside?"

Some attendants entered the scene.

"My lord," an attendant said.

The Lord Cardinal said:

"Take up those lights; there was a thicker darkness when they first came here.

"May the peace of a fair soul keep with my noble brother."

The Lord Cardinal and the servants, carrying the lights, exited.

As they exited, the Duke said:

"May joys be with you, sir!"

Alone, he said to himself about Brancha:

"She lies alone tonight for it, and must still, although my sexual desire is hard to conquer, but I have vowed never to know her as a strumpet anymore, and I must save my oath and keep my word.

"If fury does not fail, her husband dies tonight, or at the utmost, he does not live to see the morning spent tomorrow.

"Then I will make her lawfully my own, without this sin and horror.

"Now I'm chidden, for what — sex with Brancha — I shall enjoy then unforbidden after I marry her. And I'll not freeze in rooms heated with stoves: I will be able to enjoy sex with Brancha and not have to refrain from having sex with her.

"It is only a while.

"Live like a hopeful bridegroom, chaste from sex and flesh.

"And pleasure then will seem new, fair, and fresh."

The Duke was behaving like King David, who wanted to have sex with Bathsheba, and so he arranged that her husband, Uriah, would die. See 2 Samuel 11.

2 Samuel 11:26-27 (King James Version) states:

26) *And when the wife of Uriah heard that Uriah her husband was dead, she mourned for her husband.*

27) *And when the mourning was past, David sent and fetched her to his house, and she became his wife, and bare him a son. But the thing that David had done displeased the Lord.*

Alone, Hippolito said to himself:

"The morning so far wasted, yet Leantio's baseness so impudent! See if the very sun does not blush at him!

"Dare he do thus much and know that I am alive!

"Assuming that one must be vicious and commit sin, as I know that I myself am monstrously guilty, there's a blind time — the hours of darkness — made for vice. If he would use only that blind time, his affair with my sister would be conscionable and tolerable.

"Artifice, silence, secrecy and concealment, subtle cunning, and darkness are fit for such a business; but there's no pity to be bestowed on an open, obvious, and apparent sinner, an impudent daylight lecher."

Hippolito was concerned only with appearance. To him, "honor" was reputation, not virtue.

Hippolito continued:

"The great zeal that I bring to Livia's advancement in this marriage match with Lord Vincentio, as the Duke has wrought it, to the perpetual honor of our house, puts fire into my blood to purge the air of this corruption, for fear it will spread too far and poison the whole hopes of this fair fortune.

"I love her good so dearly that no brother shall venture farther for a sister's glory than I for her preferment — her advancement by making a good marriage."

Leantio and a page entered the scene.

A page is a boy-servant.

Leantio said:

"Once again I'll see that glistening whore, who shines like a serpent now that the court sun's upon her."

He was talking about his wife, Brancha.

He called:

"Page!"

"At once, sir!" the page responded.

Leantio said, "I'll go in state, too. See that the coach is ready. I'll hurry away immediately."

The page exited.

Hippolito said:

"Yes, you shall hurry, and the devil shall hurry after you. Take that at your setting forth."

Hippolito struck Leantio, and then he said:

"Now, if you'll draw, we are on equal terms, sir.

"Thou took advantage of my name in honor, upon my sister; I never saw the stroke come, until I found my reputation bleeding; and therefore I account it no sin to valor to serve thy lust so — to strike thee without warning. Now that we are of even hand — now that we are in the same position — take your best course of action against me.

"You must die."

Leantio said:

"How closely envy sticks to a man's happiness! When I was poor and cared little for life, I had no such means offered me to die: No man's wrath paid any attention to me."

Drawing his sword, he said:

"Slave, I turn this to thee to call thee to account, for a wound lately of a base stamp — a base nature — made upon me."

The base stamp was the blow that Hippolito had just given to him.

A base stamp can be 1) a base blow, or 2) a false stamp or impression on a counterfeit coin.

Coins were made of silver and gold, not of base metal.

The wound was a loss of honor: Leantio was sleeping with Hippolito's sister and so Hippolito had hit him without warning.

Hippolito said:

"It was most fitting for a base mettle."

"Mettle" can mean character, and it is a homonym of "metal."

Hippolito continued:

"Come and fetch a wound now more noble then; for I will treat thee fairer than thou have done thy soul, or our honor."

They fought, and Hippolito mortally wounded Leantio.

Hippolito then said:

"And there I think the wound is for thee."

People called, "Help! Help! Oh, part them!"

Leantio fell and said:

"False wife! I feel now thou prayed heartily for me."

He thought that Brancha had prayed for him to be murdered.

He then said:

"Rise, strumpet, by my fall; thy lust may reign now. My heartstring, and the marriage knot that tied thee, break both together."

Brancha could rise socially by becoming the wife of the Duke.

Leantio died.

Hippolito said, "There I heard the sound of your heartstring breaking, and I never liked a musical string better than that."

Guardiano, Livia, Isabella, the Foolish Ward, and Sordido entered the scene.

Livia said, "It is my brother! Are you hurt, sir?"

"Not anything," Hippolito said. "Not at all."

"Blessed fortune!" Livia said. "Shift for thyself: Take care! Escape!"

Dueling was illegal, and in this duel, someone had died.

She looked at the body, and suspecting the truth, she asked, "Who is the man thou have killed?"

"Our honor's enemy," Hippolito said.

"Do you know this man, lady?" Guardiano asked.

Livia replied:

"Leantio! My love's joy!"

She said to Hippolito, her brother:

"May wounds stick upon thee as deadly as thy sins! Are thou not hurt — may the devil take that fortune! — and he dead?

"May plagues drop into thy bowels silently and without warning, secret and fearful!"

Livia then said to the others who were present:

"Run for officers.

"Let Hippolito be apprehended with all speed, for fear he escapes and gets away. Lay hands on him.

"We cannot be too careful; it is willful murder."

Some men seized Hippolito.

Livia said to those who had seized Hippolito:

"You do Heaven's vengeance, and you do the law just service.

"You others don't know him as I do; he's a villain, as monstrous as an unnatural prodigy, and as much to be dreaded."

A "prodigy" is 1) a monster, or 2) a deformed infant, or 3) a bad omen or portent.

Hippolito said to her, "Will you just entertain a noble patience, until you just hear the reason, worthy sister?"

Livia said:

"The reason! That's a jest Hell falls to laughing at.

"Is there a reason found for the destruction of our more lawful loves; and was there none to kill the black lust between thy niece and thee, which has been kept secret so long?"

Livia believed that her relationship with Leantio was more lawful than the incestuous relationship of Hippolito and his niece: Isabella.

Shocked, Guardiano said, "What's that, good madam?"

Livia said:

"It is too true, sir.

"There she — Isabella — stands; let her deny it. The deed cries shortly in the midwife's arms unless the parents' sins strike it stillborn."

Isabella was pregnant, and her baby would be evidence of incest, unless it died at birth because its parents' sins were so evil.

Livia continued:

"And if you are not deaf and willfully ignorant, you'll hear strange new notes — the crying of an infant — before long."

She said to Isabella:

"Look at me, wench!

"It was I who betrayed thy honor cunningly to him by telling thee a false tale."

Livia had lied to Isabella when she told Isabella that she and her uncle, Hippolito, were not biologically related.

Livia continued:

"It alights upon me now.

"His arm has paid me home — in full — upon thy breast, my sweet beloved Leantio!"

Livia had been treacherous, and now treachery had been visited upon her.

Guardiano said to himself, "Was my judgment and care in choice so devilishly abused, so beyond shamefully! All the world will grin at me!"

Like Hippolito, Guardiano was concerned with appearances.

The Foolish Ward said, "Oh, Sordido! Sordido! I'm damned! I'm damned!"

"Damned!" Sordido said. "Why, sir?"

The Foolish Ward said, "I am one of the wicked! Don't you see it? I am a cuckold, a plain reprobate — wicked — cuckold."

He was right in thinking that he was a cuckold, but cuckolds are sinned against. A cuckold is not necessarily wicked.

Sordido said, "Nay, if you are damned for that, be of good cheer, sir. You will have gallant company from all professions; I'll have a wife next Sunday, too, because I'll go along with you to Hell, myself."

A proverb stated, "Who will have a handsome wife, let him choose her upon Saturday and not upon Sunday."

Sunday was the day when young women went to church to flirt rather than to worship God. They were dressed in their best clothes and looked their best.

A young woman who looks pretty on Saturday will be pretty each day of the week.

The Foolish Ward said, "That will be some comfort yet."

Livia said to Guardiano:

"You, sir, who bear your load of injuries, as I bear my load of sorrows, lend me your grieved strength to lift up this sad burden" — she pointed to the body of Leantio — "who in life performed actions than which flames were not nimbler and were not more energetic."

These actions may have been sexual.

Livia continued:

"We will talk of things that may have the luck to break our hearts together."

Guardiano said, "I'll listen to nothing but revenge and anger, whose counsels I will follow."

Livia and Guardiano exited. Guardiano carried the body of Leantio.

Sordido said, "A wife, said he! Here's a sweet plum-tree of your guardianer's grafting!"

A "plum-tree" is a vulva.

A gardener can attempt to graft a branch from one tree upon another tree.

Guardiano had attempted to graft the Foolish Ward and Isabella — two unlike people — together.

This could also be another kind of graft: Guardiano would have legally made money by fining the Foolish Ward if the Foolish Ward had declined to marry Isabella.

The Foolish Ward said:

"Nay, there's a worse name belongs to this fruit yet, if you could hit on it — a more open one."

The "more open" name was "open-arse," a slang name for the medlar fruit. A medlar is a pulpy apple that seems to be rotten as soon as it is ready to eat.

The Foolish Ward continued:

"For he who marries a whore, looks like a fellow bound all his lifetime to a medlar tree, and that's good stuff; it is no sooner ripe, but it looks rotten; and so do some queans at nineteen."

A "quean" is a whore.

"Rotten" can mean 1) decayed, or 2) infected with venereal disease.

The Foolish Ward continued:

"A pox on it!"

"A pox on it" is a curse. A "pox" is either the plague or syphilis.

The Foolish Ward continued:

"I thought there was some knavery astir, for something stirred in her belly the first night I lay with her."

"What!" Sordido said. "What, sir!"

The Foolish Ward said, "This Isabella is a woman brought up so courtly that she can sing, and dance, and tumble, too, I think. I'll never marry a wife again who has so many qualities — so many skills and accomplishments."

The word "tumble" can mean "do gymnastics," or "have sex."

Sordido said:

"Indeed, they are seldom good, master, for likely when they are taught so many, they will have one trick more of their own finding out.

"Well, give me a wench with just one good quality, to lie with none but her husband, and that's bringing up enough for any woman breathing."

"This was the fault when she was tendered to me to be my wife," the Foolish Ward said. "You never looked to this."

The fault was that Isabella was unfaithful; she was already sleeping with Hippolito.

Sordido said:

"Alas! how would you have me see through a great farthingale, sir?

A farthingale is a voluminous article of women's clothing. Skirts that were made voluminous with hoops could hide figure flaws.

Sordido continued:

"I cannot peep through a millstone, or in the going, to see what's done in the bottom."

"Going" means "moving," and the "bottom" is underneath the millstone.

Figuratively applied to women, "going" means "walking," and "bottom" means "crotch."

The Foolish Ward said:

"Her father praised her breast; she'd had the voice, indeed!

"I marveled that she sang so small indeed, being no maiden."

He may have meant that Isabella was not a young girl, and so he had expected her to have a deeper voice.

The Foolish Ward continued:

"Now I perceive there's a young chorister in her belly."

Isabella had a small voice: She was a small woman. But now the Foolish Ward was saying that he thought that the small voice was that of a fetus in her womb.

The Foolish Ward continued:

"This breeds a singing in my head, I'm sure."

"A singing in [the] head" was supposed to be a symptom of cuckoldry.

Sordido said:

"It is just the tune of your wife's cinquepace danced in a featherbed."

Literally, a cinquepace is a lively dance. Figuratively, it is a lively bout of sex.

Sordido said:

"Indeed, go lie down, master; but take heed that your cuckold's horns do not make holes in the pillowcases."

He then said to himself:

"I would not batter brows with him for a hogshead of angels: a barrel of gold coins. He would prick my skull as full of holes as a scrivener's sandbox."

Scriveners used a perforated box filled with sand to blot ink.

The Foolish Ward and Sordido exited.

Isabella said to herself about Livia:

"Was ever a maiden so cruelly beguiled to the ruin of life, soul, and honor, all of which were murdered and destroyed by one woman! I'd like to bring her name no nearer to my blood — my kinship — than Woman, and even our both being women is too much kinship. Oh, shame and horror!

"In that small distance from yonder man to me, lies sin enough to make a whole world perish."

She then said to Hippolito:

"It is time we parted, sir, and left the sight of one another. Nothing can be worse than our seeing each other to hinder repentance; for our very eyes are far more poisonous to religion than basilisks are poisonous to our eyes."

A basilisk is a half-cock and half-serpent mythological monster. Just looking into a basilisk's eyes can kill a person.

Isabella continued:

"If any goodness rests in you, hope of comforts, fear of judgments, then my request is that I never may see you anymore, and so I turn myself away from you everlastingly.

"So it is my hope to miss you."

Isabella hoped to miss meeting Hippolito everlastingly in Hell.

Isabella then said to herself:

"But as for Livia, who dared so to dally with a sin so dangerous, and lay a snare so spitefully for my youth, if the least means and smallest opportunity just favor my revenge so that I may practice the like cruel cunning upon Livia's life, as she has on my honor, I'll enact it without pity."

Isabella wanted to avoid being damned everlastingly to Hell with Hippolito, but she also wanted to enact revenge on Livia.

Hippolito said:

"Here's a care of reputation, and a sister's fortune sweetly rewarded by her."

Hippolito still thought that he had upheld his sister's honor by killing Leantio.

He continued:

"I wish that a silence, as great as that which keeps among the graves, had everlastingly chained up her tongue.

"My love for Livia has made my love for Isabella — and has made Isabella — miserable."

Guardiano and Livia entered the scene. They did not immediately go over to the others who were present.

Guardiano whispered to Livia, "If only you can dissemble your heart's griefs now! Be just a woman so far."

Many people in this society thought that women were expert dissemblers. Guardiano wanted Livia to hide her grief at the murder of Leantio.

Livia whispered to Guardiano, "Peace! Silence! I'll strive to do it, sir."

Guardiano whispered to Livia:

"Do it just as I can wear my injuries in a smile.

"Here's an occasion offered that gives anger both liberty and safety to perform things worth the fire that anger holds, without the fear of danger, or of law.

"For evils enacted under the privilege of a marriage triumph at the Duke's hasty nuptials will be thought things entirely accidental, as if all by chance, and not begotten of their own natures — not deliberately done."

A marriage triumph is a lavish entertainment held to celebrate an important marriage.

The marriage triumph would offer a kind of immunity — privilege — in that it would be easier to get away with murder because of all the activity going on to celebrate the great marriage.

Livia whispered to Guardiano:

"I understand you, sir, even to a longing for performance of it. And here behold some fruits —"

"Longing" and "performance" can refer to sex, and the "fruits" can refer to the children resulting from sex.

Livia and Guardiano went over to the others.

Livia knelt and said to Hippolito and Isabella:

"Forgive me, both of you. What I am now, having returned to sense and judgment, is not the same rage and distraction presented recently to you.

"That rude form has gone forever.

"I am now myself, I who now speak all peace and friendship; and these tears are the true springs — fountains and outward signs — of hearty penitent sorrow for those foul wrongs with which my forgetful fury slandered your virtues."

She then said about Guardiano:

"This gentleman is well resolved — satisfied — now."

Guardiano said:

"I was never otherwise.

"I knew — alas! — that it was only your anger that spoke it, and I never thought about it anymore."

Hippolito said to Livia, "Please rise, good sister."

Livia stood up.

Isabella said to herself:

"Here's even as sweet amends made for a wrong now, as one who gives a wound, and pays the surgeon. All the pain is considered nothing; the great loss of blood, and time of hindrance and incapacity are considered nothing.

"Well, I had a mother, and I can dissemble, too."

In other words: Isabella had inherited the ability to dissemble from her mother.

Isabella said out loud to Livia:

"What wrongs have slipped through anger's ignorance, aunt, my heart forgives."

Guardiano said, "Why, this is tuneful now!"

But he may have also thought, *Why thus tuneful now?*

Hippolito said, "And what I did, sister, was all for honor's cause, which time to come will prove and demonstrate to you."

Livia said:

"Being awakened to goodness, I understand so much, sir, and I praise now the fortune of your arm, and of your safety."

Hippolito had successfully killed Leantio, and Hippolito was still alive.

Livia continued:

"For by his death, you've rid me of a sin as costly to my spiritual health as any ever woman doted on.

"It has pleased the Duke so well, too, that — look at this paper, sir — he has sent you here your pardon, which I kissed with most affectionate comfort. When it was brought, then was my fit just passed. It came so well, I thought, to gladden my heart."

She handed Hippolito the pardon.

"I see his grace thinks about me," Hippolito said.

"There's no talk now but of the preparation for the great marriage of the Duke and Brancha," Livia said.

"Does he marry her, then?" Hippolito asked.

Livia said:

"With all speed, suddenly, as fast as cost can be laid on with many thousand hands.

"This gentleman — Guardiano — and I had once a purpose to have honored the first marriage of the Duke with an invention — a literary composition — of Guardiano's own.

"It was ready, the pains and effort well past, and most of the expenses paid for it."

Livia turned to Isabella and said:

"Then came the death of your good mother, niece, and turned the glory of it all to black and mourning."

Livia then faced everyone and said:

"It is a device — a masque — that would fit these times so well, too. Everything in art's treasury is not better than this masque will be. If you'll join, it shall be done; the cost shall all be mine."

A masque is an entertainment in which the performers wear masks.

Hippolito said, "You've my voice — my support — first; it will well demonstrate my thankfulness for the Duke's love and favor."

"What do you say, niece?" Livia asked Isabella.

"I am content to play one of the parts," Isabella said.

Guardiano said:

"The plot's full then."

This meant 1) the cast is full, and 2) the revenge plot planned by Guardiano and Livia is prepared.

Guardiano continued:

"Your pages, madam, will be cupids."

Cupid shoots arrows at people to make them fall in love.

"That they shall, sir," Livia said.

"You'll play your old part still: the one you were supposed to play before Isabella's mother died," Guardiano said.

"What role is it?" Livia said. "Truly, I have completely forgotten it."

Guardiano said, "Why, Juno Pronuba, the goddess of marriage."

Juno was the wife of Jupiter, king of the gods. He had many affairs with mortal women and immortal goddesses, and she was a jealous wife who took revenge on many of the women he slept with.

The Latin infinitive *nubere* means "to be married."

"Juno Pronuba" means "Juno, arranger of marriages."

"It is right indeed," Livia said.

Guardiano said to Isabella, "And you shall play the nymph who offers sacrifice to love's altar to appease Juno's wrath."

"Sacrifice, good sir?" Isabella asked.

"Must I be appeased then?" Livia asked.

"That's as you choose yourself, as you see cause," Guardiano said.

"I think it would show the more state and dignity in her deity, to be incensed and enraged," Livia said.

Juno was frequently angry. Her anger is one reason it took Aeneas so long in his travels to reach Italy, where he became an important ancestor of the Romans.

Incense played a role in some sacrifices, including the one to be performed in the masque.

Isabella said:

"It would! But my sacrifice shall take a course to appease you —"

She then said to herself:

"— or I'll fail in it and teach a sinful bawd to play a goddess."

Isabella exited.

Guardiano said to Hippolito:

"As for our parts, we'll not be ambitious, sir.

"Will it please you to walk in and see the project — the plot of the masque — that I have written down, and then take your choice of roles."

"I don't care, as long as I have a part," Hippolito said.

Everyone except Livia exited.

Alone, Livia said to herself:

"How so much trouble I have to restrain my fury from breaking into curses! Oh, how painful it is to keep great sorrow smothered!

"Surely, I think, it is harder to dissemble grief than love.

"Leantio, here in my heart the weight of thy loss lies, which nothing but destruction can suffice."

She exited.

Hautboys, which are similar to oboes, sounded.

The Duke and Brancha entered in great state, very richly attired, and attended by lords, cardinals, ladies, and others.

As they walked solemnly, the Lord Cardinal entered in a rage, and interrupted the ceremony.

The Lord Cardinal shouted:

"Cease! Cease! Religious honors done to sin disparage virtue's reverence, and they will pull Heaven's thunder upon Florence.

"Holy ceremonies were made for sacred uses, not for sinful.

"Are these the fruits of your repentance, brother? Better it had been you had never sorrowed than to abuse the benefit and return to worse than where sin left you.

"Vowed you then never to keep strumpet more, and are you now so swift in your desires to knit your honor and your life fast to her in marriage?

"Isn't sin sure and inevitable enough to wretched man, but he must bind himself in chains to it?

"Worse! Must marriage, that immaculate and unblemished robe of honor, which renders virtue glorious, fair, and fruitful to her Great Master — God — be now made the garment of leprosy and foulness?"

Leprosy — a skin disease — was associated with syphilis. Here, it means "sin."

The Lord Cardinal continued:

"Is this penitence to sanctify hot lust? What is it otherwise than worship done to devils? Is this the best amending that sin can make after her riotous behavior?

"As if a drunkard, to appease Heaven's wrath, should offer up his surfeit — his vomit — for a sacrifice: If that is comely and decent, then lust's offerings are on wedlock's sacred altar."

The Duke said:

"Here you're bitter without cause, brother.

"What I vowed to keep, I do keep as safe as you keep your conscience, and this reproach is not needed. I taste more wrath in it than I do religion, and I taste more malice in it than goodness.

"The path I tread now is honest, and it leads to lawful love, which virtue in her strictness would not check and rebuke.

"I vowed no more to keep a woman just for sensual purposes. It is done. My vow is kept because I intend to make a lawful wife of her."

The Lord Cardinal said:

"He who taught you that craft — the Devil — don't call him master long because he will undo and ruin you.

Antonio in William Shakespeare's *The Merchant of Venice* said, "The devil can cite Scripture for his purpose."

The Lord Cardinal continued:

"Don't grow too cunning for your soul, good brother.

"Is it enough to commit adulterous thefts and then take sanctuary in marriage?

"I grant that as long as an offender keeps close in a privileged temple, his life's safe. But if he ever ventures to come out, and so be taken, then he surely dies for it."

In the Middle Ages, criminals could take refuge and find sanctuary in a church. As long as they were in the church, they could not be arrested.

The Lord Cardinal continued:

"So now at this moment you're safe, but when you leave this body, Man's only privileged temple upon earth, in which the guilty soul takes sanctuary, then you will perceive what wrongs chaste vows endure, when lust usurps the bed that should be pure."

One's body is the temple of the soul; when one dies and exits the body, then one can be punished for sin.

1 Corinthians 3:16-17 (King James Version) states:

16) *Know ye not that ye are the temple of God, and that the Spirit of God dwelleth in you?*

17) *If any man defile the temple of God, him shall God destroy; for the temple of God is holy, which temple ye are.*

Brancha said:

"Sir, I have closely studied you all this while in silence, and I find great knowledge in you, and it is severe, serious, censorious learning.

"Yet among all your virtues I do not see charity written, which some call the first-born of religion, and I marvel that I cannot see it in yours."

Christian charity is love, and it is generosity of spirit.

Brancha continued:

"Believe it, sir, there is no other virtue that can be sooner missed, or later welcomed; it begins the rest, and sets them all in order."

1 Corinthians 13:13 states, *And now abideth faith, hope, charity, these three; but the greatest of these is charity*" (King James Version).

Brancha continued:

"Heaven and angels take great delight in a converted sinner."

Luke 15:10 states, *Likewise, I say unto you, there is joy in the presence of the angels of God over one sinner that repenteth*" (King James Version).

Brancha continued:

"Why should you then, a servant who professes to be a Christian, differ so much from them? If every woman who commits evil should be therefore kept back in desires of goodness, how should virtue be known and honored? To take a burning taper from a man who is blind is no wrong. He never misses it, but to take light from one who sees, that's injury and spite.

"Please tell me whether religion is better served when lives that are licentious are made honest, or when they still run through a sinful blood — a sinful desire?

"It is nothing virtue's temples to deface ...

"But to build on the ruins and restore the temple, there's a work of grace."

The Duke could "build on the ruins" by marrying Brancha and making her an honest woman.

The Duke said to Brancha:

"I kiss thee for that spirit; thou have praised thy wit in a modest way."

She had spoken sensibly while being polite to the Lord Cardinal.

The Duke then said to the musicians:

"On, on there!"

The hautboys sounded.

Everyone exited except the Lord Cardinal.

Alone, the Lord Cardinal said to himself, "Lust is bold, and it will have divine vengeance speak before it is controlled and put down."

He exited.

CHAPTER 5

— 5.1 —

Guardiano and the Foolish Ward spoke together about the upcoming masque and the revenge plot.

Guardiano said, "Speak, have thou any sense of thy abuse? Do thou know what wrong's done to thee?"

The Foolish Ward said, "I would be an ass if I did not know. I cannot wash my face without feeling my forehead."

The Foolish Ward was feeling his forehead for the invisible horns of a cuckold — he knew that he was a cuckold.

If he lacked the intelligence to know that he was a cuckold, then he would be an ass.

Guardiano handed the Foolish Ward a caltrop and said:

"Here, take this caltrop and convey it secretly into the place I showed you."

A caltrop is a weapon: an iron ball with four spikes, constructed in such a way that one spike always faced upward when the caltrop was placed on the ground.

Guardiano pointed to a trapdoor and continued:

"Look, sir, this is the trapdoor to it."

"I know it of old, uncle, since the last triumph — that is, the last pageant," the Foolish Ward said. "Here rose up a devil with one eye, I remember, with a company of fireworks at his tail."

Some old-fashioned plays included a devil and firecrackers.

Guardiano said:

"Please stop squibbing now."

"Squibbing" is "talking foolishly."

A "squib" is a "firecracker."

Guardiano continued:

"Listen closely to me, and don't fail when thou hear me give a stamp with my foot to open the trapdoor; the villain's caught then."

The Foolish Ward said:

"If I miss you, hang me."

He meant: If I miss your signal, hang me.

The Foolish Ward continued:

"I love to catch a villain, and your stamp shall go current, I promise you."

The stamp is of Guardiano's foot, but coins were stamped with an image; if a coin was current, it was legal tender.

The Foolish Ward continued:

"But how shall I rise up and let him down, too, all at one hole?"

Hmm. "Rise up"? "Let him down"? "One hole"? Say no more.

The Foolish Ward continued:

"That will be a horrible puzzle."

The Foolish Ward was talking about rising up out of the trap door at the same time that Hippolito was coming down.

The Foolish Ward continued:

"You know I have a part in the masque; I play Slander."

Guardiano replied, "True, but never make you ready for it. You needn't dress for the part."

Guardiano wanted to kill Hippolito before the Foolish Ward appeared as Slander.

"No?" the Foolish Ward said. "My clothes and all are bought, and I have a foul fiend's head with a long contumelious tongue in the chaps — the jaws — of it, a very fit shape for Slander in the parishes outside London."

"Contumelious" means "offensive." The Foolish Ward has an excellent vocabulary.

"It shall not come so far," Guardiano said. "The masque will not be performed long enough for your character to appear in it. Thou don't understand it."

"Oh! Oh!" the Foolish Ward said.

Guardiano said, "He shall be deep enough before that time, and stick first upon those points of the caltrop."

"Now I understand you, guardianer," the Foolish Ward said.

Guardiano said, "Leave, and listen for the privy — secret — stamp — that's all thy part."

The Foolish Ward said, "Stamp my horns in a mortar if I miss you and your signal and give the powder in white wine to sick cuckolds, a very present and immediate remedy for the headache."

Some medicines of the time included powered horn dissolved in white wine.

Cuckolds had headaches because of their horns.

The Foolish Ward exited.

Alone, Guardiano said to himself:

"If this should in any way miscarry now — although if the fool is nimble and alert enough, it is certain to succeed — the pages who represent the swift-winged cupids have been taught to hit Hippolito with their shafts of love, befitting his part."

Hippolito will play the part of a love-struck shepherd.

Guardiano continued:

"I have cunningly poisoned those shafts of love.

"Hippolito cannot escape my fury; and those ills will all be blamed on fortune and luck, not our wills. That's all the sport of it! For who will imagine ...

"That at the celebration of this night ...

"Any mischance that happens can flow from spite?"

He exited.

Trumpets sounded.

The Duke, Brancha, the Lord Cardinal, Fabritio, and other cardinals, and lords and ladies in state entered. They were in a balcony above the stage the masque would be performed on.

The Duke said to Brancha, whom he had married, "Now, our fair Duchess, your delight shall witness how you're beloved and honored; all the glories bestowed upon the gladness of this night are done for your bright sake."

Brancha said, "I am the more in debt, my lord, to loves and courtesies that offer up themselves so bounteously to do me honored grace, without my merit."

A theological debate concerned how people are spiritually saved. Is it through divine grace or through merit that shows itself in things such as good deeds?

The Duke said:

"A goodness set in greatness! How it sparkles afar off like pure diamonds set in gold!

"How perfect and complete my desires would be if I could witness just a fair noble peace between your two spirits!"

The two spirits were Brancha's and the Lord Cardinal's.

The Duke continued:

"The reconciliation would be sweeter to me than longer life is to him who fears to die."

He then said to the Lord Cardinal:

"Good sir."

The Lord Cardinal said, "I profess peace, and I am content."

"I'll see the seal upon it, and then it is firm," the Duke said.

In this society, documents were sealed with wax, which was imprinted with insignia such as a coat of arms.

The phrase "seal with a kiss" was well-known. This was a kiss of reconciliation.

"You shall have all you wish," the Lord Cardinal said.

He kissed Brancha.

The Duke said, "I have all indeed now."

Brancha said to herself:

"But I have made surer work; this show of reconciliation shall not blind me.

"He who begins so early to reprove and criticize — quickly get rid of him, or else look for little love from him. Beware a brother-in-law's malice; he's the next heir, too."

Brancha may give birth to an heir who will inherit the Dukedom, pushing aside the Lord Cardinal, who was now next in line to inherit the Dukedom.

Brancha continued saying to herself:

"Cardinal, you die this night; the plot's laid surely and securely.

"In time of entertainments, death may steal in securely because then it is least thought on.

"For he who is most religious, holy friend Lord Cardinal, does not at all hours think upon his end. He has his times of frailty, and his thoughts, their transports and raptures, too, through flesh and blood ...

"For all his zeal, his learning, and his light,

"As well as we, poor soul Lord Cardinal, who sin by night."

In other words: The Lord Cardinal, despite his profession, has carnal thoughts like the rest of us.

The Lord Cardinal's "light" is his enlightenment.

Fabritio gave the Duke a paper.

"What's this, Fabritio?" the Duke asked.

Fabritio answered, "By the Virgin Mary, my lord, the model — the plot summary — of what's going to be presented."

The Duke said:

"Oh, we thank their loves."

The people participating in the performance seemed to be showing respect to the Duke.

The Duke continued:

"Sweet Duchess, take your seat; listen to the subject matter of the masque."

He then read the description of the masque out loud:

"*There is a nymph who haunts the woods and springs,*

"*In love with two at once, and they with her;*

"*Equal it runs; but to decide these things,*

"*The cause [case] to mighty Juno they refer,*

"*She being the marriage-goddess: the two lovers*

"They offer sighs; the nymph [offers] a sacrifice;

"All to please Juno, who by signs discovers [reveals]

"How the event [outcome] shall be, so that strife dies:

"Then springs a second [strife]; for the man refused [not allowed to be with the nymph]

"Grows discontent, and out of love abused [frustrated],

"He raises Slander up, like a black fiend,

"To disgrace the other, who pays him ill end."

In the last line, "who" refers to "the other lover."

Brancha said:

"Truly, my lord, this is a pretty pleasing plot, and fits the occasion well.

"Envy and Slander are things soon raised against two faithful lovers. But the comfort is that they're not long unrewarded."

The two lovers are not long unrewarded. The lover who raises Envy and Slander gets his just rewards: He is killed. The other lover gets the nymph.

Music played.

The Duke said, "This music shows they're making their entrance now."

Brancha said to herself, "Then enter all my wishes."

Three actors performing these roles entered the scene:

1) Hymen, the god of marriage, wearing a yellow robe.

2) Ganymede, the cupbearer to Jupiter, king of the gods. Ganymede was wearing a blue robe sprinkled with stars.

3) Hebe, another cupbearer and the goddess of youth and spring, who was wearing a white robe with golden stars.

The three actors had covered cups — cups with attached lids — in their hands. They put the cups on a table, they danced a short dance, and then they bowed to the Duke and the rest of the company.

Hymen spoke, addressing himself to Brancha, "To thee, fair bride, Hymen offers up this celestial cup of nuptial joys. Taste it, and thou shall forever find love in thy bed and peace in thy mind."

Taking the cup, Brancha said. "We'll taste it for you, to be sure; it would be a pity to disgrace so pretty a beginning."

"It was spoken nobly," the Duke said.

Ganymede said:

"Two cups of nectar, the drink of the gods, have we begged from Jove.

"Hebe, give that cup to innocence; I will give this cup to love."

Hebe stumbled and then picked up a cup.

Hebe gave a cup to the Lord Cardinal, and Ganymede gave a cup to the Duke.

Brancha, the Duke, and the Lord Cardinal drank.

As events would show, Hebe had picked up a different cup than the one Brancha wanted her to pick up. Brancha had poisoned the wine, hoping to kill the Lord Cardinal.

Ganymede said, "Take heed of stumbling anymore; look where you are going. Remember still the Via Lactea — the Milky Way."

According to a fable, Hebe had been cupbearer to Jupiter before Ganymede, but she stumbled and spilled the milk, creating the Milky Way, and so lost her job.

Hebe replied, "Well, Ganymede, you have more faults, although not as well known as my one fault; I spilled one cup, but you have filched many cups."

"No more," Hymen said. "Stop arguing for Hymen's sake. In love we met, and so let's part."

The actors exited.

The Duke said:

"But wait! Here's no such persons in the plot summary as these three: Hymen, Hebe, and Ganymede.

"The actors whom this plot summary here reveals are only four — Juno, a nymph, and two lovers."

Those four were the main roles; there were also some lesser roles.

Brancha said:

"This is some ante-masque, a short masque presented before the main masque, perhaps, my lord, to entertain us and while away the time."

She said to herself:

"Now that my peace is perfect and complete, let entertainment come on apace."

Bianca had arranged for the ante-masque to be presented. Her peace was perfect and complete because she was now married to the Duke and because she thought that the plot she had formed would succeed.

Brancha then said out loud:

"Now is the time for the actors in the main masque, my lord."

Music played.

Brancha said:

"Listen! You can hear the music from them."

"The nymphs indeed!" the Duke said.

Two masquers entered, dressed like nymphs, bearing two lit candles. Then came Isabella, dressed as another nymph with flowers and garlands, carrying a censor with fire in it. They set the censor and candles on Juno's altar with much reverence.

The three nymphs sang this song in parts, with Isabella singing one part, and the two other nymphs singing the rest:

"Juno, nuptial goddess,

"Thou who rules over coupled bodies,

"Ties man to woman, never to forsake her,

"Thou only powerful marriage-maker,

"Pity this amazed [perplexed] affection;

"I love both, and both love me;

"Nor know I where to give rejection,

"My heart likes [them] so equally,

"Until thou set right my peace of life,

"And with thy power conclude this strife."

Apparently, Isabella sang the last five lines of the song.

Isabella said to the two nymphs:

"Now, with my thanks, depart to the springs where you live; I will go to these wells of love."

The two nymphs exited.

Isabella's character then prayed to Juno:

"Thou sacred goddess, and queen of nuptials, daughter to great Saturn, sister and wife to Jove, imperial Juno, pity this passionate conflict in my breast, this long war between two affections. Crown me with victory, and my heart's at peace."

Juno was both Jupiter's sister and his wife.

Hippolito and Guardiano, dressed like shepherds, entered the scene.

They were playing the two shepherds in love with the nymph.

"Make me that happy man, thou mighty goddess," Hippolito said.

"But I live most in hope, if truest love merits the greatest comfort," Guardiano said.

Isabella said, "I love both with such an even and fair affection, I don't know which to speak for, which to wish for, until thou, Juno, great arbitress, between lovers' hearts, by thy auspicious grace, designate the man. Juno, your pity I implore."

"We all implore it," Hippolito and Guardiano said.

Stage machinery lowered Livia, who was attired like Juno, from above and suspended her above the altar on which Isabella will burn incense. Livia was attended by cupids with arrows.

Isabella said:

"And after sighs, contrition's truest odors, I offer to thy powerful deity this precious incense."

She scattered incense on the fire.

Isabella continued:

"May it ascend peacefully."

The smoke of the incense rose. Isabella had poisoned it, intending to kill Livia.

Isabella said to herself:

"And if it keeps true touch — if it proves trustworthy — my good aunt Juno, it will test your immortality before much longer.

"I fear you'll never get so near to Heaven again, when you're once down."

Livia said:

"Although you and your affections seem to be compared to our illustrious brightness all as dark as night's inheritance — Hell — is, we pity you, and your requests are granted.

"You ask for signs. They shall be given you; we'll be gracious to you.

"He, of those two, whom we determine for you, love's arrows shall wound twice, the later wound betokens love in age; for so are all whose love continues firmly all their lifetime. They are twice wounded at their marriage; else affection dies when youth ends."

Livia then said to herself:

"This savor — the smell — of the incense overcomes me!"

She said out loud:

"Now for a sign of wealth and golden days, bright-eyed prosperity, which all couples love, aye, and creates love, take that."

Livia threw flaming gold — poisoned gold dust — on Isabella, who sank down, dead.

The gold dust, as it fell, looked like flames.

Livia then said:

"Our brother Jove never denies us any of his burning treasure, to express bounty."

The Duke said, "Isabella falls down upon receiving it. What's the meaning of that?"

Fabritio, Isabella's father, said, "She falls down overjoyed, perhaps. Too much prosperity overjoys us all, and she has her lapful, it seems, my lord."

"This swerves a little from the plot summary, though," the Duke said. "Look, my lords."

He pointed to a place on the plot summary.

Guardiano said to himself, "All's secure and going as planned. Now comes my part to toll — to lure — Hippolito hither to the trapdoor to his death. Then, with a stamp of my foot given, he's dispatched as cunningly as Livia dispatched Isabella."

Guardiano moved and stood over the trapdoor as he prepared to lure Hippolito there.

But Hippolito moved to where Isabella's corpse lay. Discovering that Isabella was dead, Hippolito said, "Stark dead! Oh, treachery! Cruelly made away! What's happening!"

In anger, he stamped his foot on the stage floor.

Hearing the stamp, the Foolish Ward opened the trapdoor and Guardiano fell through it.

Fabritio said, "Look, there's one of the lovers dropped away, too."

"Why, surely this plot's drawn up inaccurately," the Duke said. "No such thing as that is written here."

They were not surprised by the actors dying on stage. Tragedies of the time were filled with such "deaths."

Livia said:

"Oh, I am sick to the death! Let me down quickly! This fume is deadly! Oh, it has poisoned me!

"My cunning has achieved its desired outcome, but Isabella's art has paid me back. My own ambition pulls me down to ruin."

Livia's playing the goddess Juno may be regarded as ambition. The Greek and Roman gods played with mortal lives, and Livia had succeeded in killing Isabella.

Livia fell down and died.

Hippolito said, "Nay, then I kiss thy cold lips, and applaud this thy revenge in death."

He kissed Isabella's dead lips.

Fabritio said:

"Look, Juno's down, too. What is she doing there? Her pride should keep aloft.

"She was accustomed to scorn the earth in other shows. I think her peacock's feathers are much pulled."

Peacocks pulled Juno's chariot. Peacocks are a symbol of pride.

The cupids shot arrows at Hippolito. The arrows had been poisoned by Guardiano, but the cupids did not know that.

Poisoned by the arrows, Hippolito said, "Oh! Death runs through my blood, in a wild flame, too. A plague on those cupids! Some of you lay hold on them. Let them not escape! They have spoiled and destroyed me; the shafts are deadly."

The Duke said, "I have quite lost myself in this plot."

"My great lords, we are all confounded and destroyed," Hippolito said to the Duke and other guests.

The Duke said, "What!"

Hippolito said, "They are dead, and I am worse."

He was still alive and suffering from the poisoned arrows. Also, he was facing damnation.

Fabritio said, "Dead! My girl Isabella is dead? I hope that my sister Juno has not served me so."

Hippolito said:

"Lust and forgetfulness of virtue and morality have been among us, and we are brought to nothing.

"May some blessed charitable person lend me the speeding pity of his sword to quench this fire in my blood!

"Leantio's death has brought all this upon us — now I taste it — and made us lay plots to confound and destroy each other.

"The outcome so proves it; and man's understanding is riper at his fall, than it is all his lifetime.

"Livia in a madness for her lover's death revealed a fearful lust in the close relationship of Isabella and me, for which I am punished dreadfully and unlooked for.

"She proved to be her own ruin, too; vengeance met vengeance, like an agreed-upon set match, aka conspiracy — it was as if the plagues of sin had been agreed to meet here altogether.

"But how her fawning partner — Guardiano, who was always fawning to the Duke — fell, I don't understand, unless he was caught by some springe — some trap and snare — of his own setting, for, I swear on my pain, he never dreamed of dying.

"The plot was all his own, and he had cunning enough to save himself, but it is the property of guilty deeds to draw wise men downward, and therefore, the wonder ceases."

"Downward" means "downward to Hell."

Hippolito then said:

"Oh, this torment!"

"Our guards below there!" the Duke called.

A lord and a few guards entered the scene.

"My lord," the lord said to the Duke.

Hippolito said, "Run and meet death then, and cut off time and pain."

He ran onto and mortally wounded himself on a guard's halberd, a weapon that combines spear and axe.

The lord said to the Duke, "Behold, my lord, he's run his breast upon a weapon's point."

The Duke said:

"Upon the first night of our nuptial honors, destruction plays her triumph — her pageant — and great mischiefs wear a mask and disguise themselves as expected pleasures. It is ill-omened. They are things most fearfully ominous, and I don't like them."

He ordered the guards:

"Remove these ruined bodies from our eyesight."

The guards carried away the bodies.

Brancha said to herself, "Not yet no change? When does the Lord Cardinal fall to the earth?"

The lord gave the Duke a piece of paper and said:

"Will it just please your excellence to peruse that paper, which is a brief confession from the heart of him — Guardiano — who fell first. He wrote this confession before his soul departed, and there the darkness of these deeds speaks plainly.

"This paper tells the full scope, the manner, and the intent of his plot.

"His ward, who unintentionally let him down through the trapdoor to his death, immediately fled because of fear after hearing the voice of Guardiano and realizing that he — the ward — had made a mistake."

Brancha said to herself, still expecting the Lord Cardinal to die, "Nor yet?"

The Duke said to his brother, the Lord Cardinal, "Read! Read! For I am lost in sight and strength."

He fell.

The Lord Cardinal said, "My noble brother!"

Brancha said:

"Oh, the curse of wretchedness! My deadly hand has fallen upon my lord and husband!

"Destruction, take me to thee!"

She said to others who were blocking her way to the Duke:

"Give me passage and let me go to him. May the pains and plagues of a lost soul fall upon anyone who hinders me a moment!"

Dying, the Duke said, "My heart swells bigger yet. Help me here! Break my collar open! My breast flies open next!"

In this society, people believed that at the moment of death the blood rushed to the heart and the dying person felt as if their chest would burst.

The Duke died.

Now beside the Duke's corpse, Brancha said to the Lord Cardinal, "Oh! With the poison that was prepared for thee! For thee, Cardinal! It was meant for thee!"

The Lord Cardinal said about his dead brother, "Poor prince!"

Brancha said:

"Accursed error! Give me thy last breath, thou infected bosom, and wrap two spirits in one poisoned vapor.

"Thus, thus, reward thy murderer, and turn death into a parting kiss. My soul stands ready at my lips, even vexed to stay one minute after thee."

She kissed the lips of the dead Duke, thereby taking some of the poisoned wine on her lips.

The Lord Cardinal said, "The greatest sorrow and astonishment that ever struck the general peace of Florence dwells in this hour."

Feeling the effects of the poison, Brancha said:

"So my desires are satisfied: I feel death's power within me.

"Cursed poison, thou have somewhat prevailed in me, although thy chief force was spent in my lord's bosom, but my deformity in spirit is fouler. A blemished face best fits a leprous soul."

Brancha scratched her face with her fingernails.

She then said:

"What am I doing here? These are all strangers to me."

Brancha was from Venice, not Florence.

When she had first come to Florence, she had told Leantio's mother, "Here are my friends, and few is the number of good friends."

Brancha continued:

"They are not known to me except by their malice, now thou are gone. Nor do I seek their pities."

She grabbed the cup of poisoned wine.

The Lord Cardinal said, "Oh, restrain her ignorant, willful hand!"

Brancha drank what was left of the poisoned wine and said:

"Now do; it is done.

"Leantio, now I feel the breach of marriage at my heart-breaking — at the time of my death.

"Oh, the deadly snares that women set for women, without pity either to soul or honor! Learn by me to know your foe!

"In this belief I die: We have no enemy like our own sex ... no enemy."

In other words: Women should beware women, for their greatest enemies are other women.

The lord said to the Lord Cardinal, "See, my lord, what shift — expedient — she's made to be her own destruction."

Brancha said:

"Pride, greatness, honors, beauty, youth, ambition — you must all go down together; there's no help for it.

"Yet this is my gladness — that I remove myself from life, tasting the same death in a cup of love."

She died.

The Lord Cardinal said:

"Sin, what thou are, these ruins show too piteously.

"Two kings on one throne cannot sit together.

"But one must necessarily down, for his title's wrong.

"So where lust reigns, that prince cannot reign long."

In other words: The two kings are lust and virtue. They cannot rule together, and so lust must be dethroned.

APPENDIX A: NOTES
— 1.1 —
Original Sin

For Your Information:

Original sin is the Christian doctrine that holds that humans, through the fact of birth, inherit a tainted nature in need of regeneration and a proclivity to sinful conduct. The biblical basis for the belief is generally found in Genesis 3 (the story of the expulsion of Adam and Eve from the Garden of Eden), in a line in Psalm 51:5 ("I was brought forth in iniquity, and in sin did my mother conceive me") and in Paul's Epistle to the Romans, 5:12-21 ("Therefore, just as sin entered the world through one man, and death through sin, and in this way death came to all people, because all sinned").

Source: "Original sin." *Wikipedia.* Accessed 10 April 2023. https://en.wikipedia.org/wiki/Original_sin
For Your Information: original sin

original sin, in Christian doctrine, the condition or state of sin into which each human being is born; also, the origin (i.e., the cause, or source) of this state. Traditionally, the origin has been ascribed to the sin of the first man, Adam, who disobeyed God in eating the forbidden fruit (of knowledge of good and evil) and, in consequence, transmitted his sin and guilt by heredity to his descendants.

Source: "original sin." *Britannica.* Accessed 10 April 2023. https://www.britannica.com/topic/kerygma

— 2.2 —

Thomas More's Utopia

The Thomas More anecdote, which is retold in David Bruce's own words, comes from this source:

Vicki León, *Uppity Women of Medieval Times*, New York: MJF Books, 1997. Pp. 58-59.

— 5.2 —

Deaths and Suicides and Survivals

Brancha: Commits suicide because the Duke dies.

The Duke: Drinks poisoned wine that was prepared by Brancha for the Lord Cardinal.

The Foolish Ward: Survives.

Guardiano: Falls through trapdoor onto a caltrop when the Foolish Ward opens the trapdoor at the wrong time.

Hippolito: Poisoned by arrows that Guardiano prepared. Commits suicide because Isabella dies and because of the pain he is in from the poison.

Isabella: Dies when Livia throws flaming gold on her.

Livia: Dies because she inhales incense that was poisoned by Isabella.

The Lord Cardinal: Survives.

At least some of the characters who plan to murder other characters hope to get away with it by having everyone think that the deaths were accidental. It's hard to see how some of the deaths could be considered accidental.

Poisoned incense seems to be a bad way to kill just one person. I imagine some of the audience smelled the incense.

I don't know what "flaming gold" is. "Flaming" can mean "resembling fire." Possibly, Livia throws poisoned gold dust onto Isabella.

These myths may or may not be related to "flaming gold":

Semele was the mortal mother of the god Bacchus; Jupiter, king of the gods, was his father. He promised to give Semele anything she wanted if she would sleep with him. After they had slept together, she told him that she wanted to see him in his full divine glory rather than just in the form he took when he appeared to mortals. Because he had sworn an inviolable oath, he did as she requested. Unable to endure the sight, she burst into flames. She was already pregnant with Bacchus, but Jupiter rescued the fetus and sewed it in his thigh until it was ready to be born. Because Bacchus had been "born" from an immortal god, Bacchus was himself an immortal god.

An oracle had told Danaë's father, King Acrisius of Argos, that her son would kill him. Therefore, he kept her locked up. Jupiter, the lustful king of the gods, however, came to her in a shower of golden rain. Danaë, made pregnant by Jupiter, gave birth to the Greek hero Perseus. King Acrisius put Danaë and Perseus, her son, into a chest and threw it into the sea. Neptune, god of the sea, provided a calm sea, and the chest washed up on the western coast of Italy, where Danaë founded the city of Ardea. Perseus grew up, learned about the prophecy that he would kill his father, and resolved never to go to Argos. Unfortunately, he competed in athletic games elsewhere, his aged father watched the games, and Perseus accidentally killed him with a discus.

APPENDIX B: FAIR USE

The French Jean Le Pautre (1618-1682) created a print titled "Jupiter Appearing to Io in a Shower of Gold." It appears in *Oeuvres*, Vol. III, plate 13. Probably, Jean Le Pautre simply made a mistake in using Io instead of Danaë.

§ 107. Limitations on exclusive rights: Fair use

Release date: 2004-04-30

Notwithstanding the provisions of sections 106 and 106A, the fair use of a copyrighted work, including such use by reproduction in copies or phonorecords or by any other means specified by that section, for purposes such as criticism, comment, news reporting, teaching (including multiple copies for classroom use), scholarship, or research, is not an infringement of copyright. In determining whether the use made of a work in any particular case is a fair use the factors to be considered shall include —

(1) the purpose and character of the use, including whether such use is of a commercial nature or is for nonprofit educational purposes;

(2) the nature of the copyrighted work;

(3) the amount and substantiality of the portion used in relation to the copyrighted work as a whole; and

(4) the effect of the use upon the potential market for or value of the copyrighted work.

The fact that a work is unpublished shall not itself bar a finding of fair use if such finding is made upon consideration of all the above factors.

Source of Fair Use information:
http://www.law.cornell.edu/uscode/17/107.html

APPENDIX C: ABOUT THE AUTHOR

It was a dark and stormy night. Suddenly a cry rang out, and on a hot summer night in 1954, Josephine, wife of Carl Bruce, gave birth to a boy — me. Unfortunately, this young married couple allowed Reuben Saturday, Josephine's brother, to name their first-born. Reuben, aka "The Joker," decided that Bruce was a nice name, so he decided to name me Bruce Bruce. I have gone by my middle name — David — ever since.

Being named Bruce David Bruce hasn't been all bad. Bank tellers remember me very quickly, so I don't often have to show an ID. It can be fun in charades, also. When I was a counselor as a teenager at Camp Echoing Hills in Warsaw, Ohio, a fellow counselor gave the signs for "sounds like" and "two words," then she pointed to a bruise on her leg twice. Bruise Bruise? Oh yeah, Bruce Bruce is the answer!

Uncle Reuben, by the way, gave me a haircut when I was in kindergarten. He cut my hair short and shaved a small bald spot on the back of my head. My mother wouldn't let me go to school until the bald spot grew out again.

Of all my brothers and sisters (six in all), I am the only transplant to Athens, Ohio. I was born in Newark, Ohio, and have lived all around Southeastern Ohio. However, I moved to Athens to go to Ohio University and have never left.

At Ohio U, I never could make up my mind whether to major in English or Philosophy, so I got a bachelor's degree with a double major in both areas, then I added a Master of Arts degree in English and a Master of Arts degree in Philosophy. Yes, I have my MAMA degree.

Currently, and for a long time to come (I eat fruits and veggies), I am spending my retirement writing books such as *Nadia Comaneci: Perfect 10*, *The Funniest People in Comedy*, *Homer's* Iliad: *A Retelling in Prose*, and *William Shakespeare's* Hamlet: *A Retelling in Prose*.

If all goes well, I will publish one or two books a year for the rest of my life. (On the other hand, a good way to make God laugh is to tell Her your plans.)

By the way, my sister Brenda Kennedy writes romances such as *A New Beginning* and *Shattered Dreams*.

APPENDIX D: SOME BOOKS BY DAVID BRUCE

Retellings of a Classic Work of Literature

Arden of Faversham: A Retelling

Ben Jonson's The Alchemist: *A Retelling*

Ben Jonson's The Arraignment, or Poetaster: *A Retelling*

Ben Jonson's Bartholomew Fair: *A Retelling*

Ben Jonson's The Case is Altered: *A Retelling*

Ben Jonson's Catiline's Conspiracy: *A Retelling*

Ben Jonson's The Devil is an Ass: *A Retelling*

Ben Jonson's Epicene: *A Retelling*

Ben Jonson's Every Man in His Humor: *A Retelling*

Ben Jonson's Every Man Out of His Humor: *A Retelling*

Ben Jonson's The Fountain of Self-Love, or Cynthia's Revels: *A Retelling*

Ben Jonson's The Magnetic Lady, or Humors Reconciled: *A Retelling*

Ben Jonson's The New Inn, or The Light Heart: *A Retelling*

Ben Jonson's Sejanus' Fall: *A Retelling*

Ben Jonson's The Staple of News: *A Retelling*

Ben Jonson's A Tale of a Tub: *A Retelling*

Ben Jonson's Volpone, or the Fox: *A Retelling*

Christopher Marlowe's Complete Plays: Retellings

Christopher Marlowe's Dido, Queen of Carthage: *A Retelling*

Christopher Marlowe's Doctor Faustus: *Retellings of the 1604 A-Text and of the 1616 B-Text*

Christopher Marlowe's Edward II: *A Retelling*

Christopher Marlowe's The Massacre at Paris: *A Retelling*

Christopher Marlowe's The Rich Jew of Malta: *A Retelling*

Christopher Marlowe's Tamburlaine, Parts 1 and 2: *Retellings*

Dante's Divine Comedy: *A Retelling in Prose*

Dante's Inferno: *A Retelling in Prose*

Dante's Purgatory: *A Retelling in Prose*

Dante's Paradise: *A Retelling in Prose*

The Famous Victories of Henry V: *A Retelling*

From the Iliad *to the* Odyssey: *A Retelling in Prose of Quintus of Smyrna's* Posthomerica

George Chapman, Ben Jonson, and John Marston's Eastward Ho! *A Retelling*

George Peele's The Arraignment of Paris: *A Retelling*

George Peele's The Battle of Alcazar: *A Retelling*

George Peele's David and Bathsheba, and the Tragedy of Absalom: *A Retelling*

George Peele's Edward I: *A Retelling*

George Peele's The Old Wives' Tale: *A Retelling*

George-a-Greene: *A Retelling*
The History of King Leir: *A Retelling*
Homer's Iliad: *A Retelling in Prose*
Homer's Odyssey: *A Retelling in Prose*
J.W. Gent.'s The Valiant Scot: *A Retelling*
Jason and the Argonauts: A Retelling in Prose of Apollonius of Rhodes' Argonautica
John Ford: Eight Plays Translated into Modern English
John Ford's The Broken Heart: *A Retelling*
John Ford's The Fancies, Chaste and Noble: *A Retelling*
John Ford's The Lady's Trial: *A Retelling*
John Ford's The Lover's Melancholy: *A Retelling*
John Ford's Love's Sacrifice: *A Retelling*
John Ford's Perkin Warbeck: *A Retelling*
John Ford's The Queen: *A Retelling*
John Ford's 'Tis Pity She's a Whore: *A Retelling*
John Lyly's Campaspe: *A Retelling*
John Lyly's Endymion, The Man in the Moon: *A Retelling*
John Lyly's Galatea: *A Retelling*
John Lyly's Love's Metamorphosis: *A Retelling*
John Lyly's Midas: *A Retelling*
John Lyly's Mother Bombie: *A Retelling*
John Lyly's Sappho and Phao: *A Retelling*
John Lyly's The Woman in the Moon: *A Retelling*
John Webster's The White Devil: *A Retelling*
King Edward III: *A Retelling*
Mankind: *A Medieval Morality Play* (A Retelling)
Margaret Cavendish's The Unnatural Tragedy: *A Retelling*
The Merry Devil of Edmonton: *A Retelling*
The Summoning of Everyman: *A Medieval Morality Play* (A Retelling)
Robert Greene's Friar Bacon and Friar Bungay: *A Retelling*
The Taming of a Shrew: *A Retelling*
Tarlton's Jests: A Retelling
Thomas Middleton's A Chaste Maid in Cheapside: *A Retelling*
Thomas Middleton's Women Beware Women: *A Retelling*
Thomas Middleton and Thomas Dekker's The Roaring Girl: *A Retelling*
Thomas Middleton and William Rowley's The Changeling: *A Retelling*
The Trojan War and Its Aftermath: Four Ancient Epic Poems
Virgil's Aeneid: *A Retelling in Prose*
William Shakespeare's 5 Late Romances: Retellings in Prose
William Shakespeare's 10 Histories: Retellings in Prose
William Shakespeare's 11 Tragedies: Retellings in Prose
William Shakespeare's 12 Comedies: Retellings in Prose